$2.49
3/13

PLAYING IT RIGHT

"If you want to get your own back, you know how to do it, don't you?"

"Yeah," said Trinton, squaring up and showing his clenched fists.

"No," said Mr Bunting, "that's not the way! You go out there and beat them fair and square on the cricket field."

When Jubilee Street School cricket team piled out of the dilapidated old minibus for the match against Priory School, they were a motley crew – eleven boys in their shabby jeans and tee-shirts, challenging the Priory School in its white flannels and blazers with its fine tradition of cricket.

The odds had been against the Jubilee Street team all the way. With no playing field, poor equipment, bitter rivalry among the boys and opposition from the teachers it had been hard to organize team practices. Prospects looked even grimmer when Colin and Trinton, two of the star players, were banned from the team on suspicion of burglary.

Despite all these setbacks, the boys in the Jubilee Street team were determined to prove their worth – not only at cricket.

This exciting but realistic story, which brilliantly catches the tensions and humour of the boys and teachers in a junior school, was chosen as the runner-up in the Collins' competition for children's books for multi-ethnic Britain.

Playing It Right

Tony Drake

Collins

William Collins Sons & Co Ltd
London · Glasgow · Sydney · Auckland
Toronto · Johannesburg

Quotation from *Islands* by Edward Brathwaite,
© Oxford University Press 1969,
by permission of the Oxford University Press

First published 1979
© Tony Drake 1979

ISBN 0 00 184630 2

Made and printed in Great Britain by
William Collins Sons & Co Ltd, Glasgow

this isn't no time for playin'
the fool nor makin' no sport; this is cricket!

Edward Brathwaite

1

The notice appeared just after the Easter holiday on the stone staircase that led up to the main hall of Jubilee Street Middle School.

SCHOOL CRICKET

I am hoping to run a school cricket team this term. Would any boys who wish to take part please meet at the boys' changing room on Tuesday, April 14th, immediately after scnool, for a preliminary practice? White plimsolls and a white shirt are essential.

F.R. Bunting

It was pinned neatly to the green baize noticeboard, between one poster warning of the danger of Colorado Beetles to the potato crop and another advertising last year's jumble sale.

The first of the boys to see the notice was Colin Tremaine. As usual, on that day of the week, 4C had music last lesson of the day. As usual, Colin got into trouble with the music teacher, Miss Ringrose: this time for talking through one of the quiet bits of the classical record she was playing.

"Out!" she shouted at him. "Go and stand by the headmaster's door. I will NOT have you disrupting my lessons."

Colin did not go quietly. He kicked his chair over and slammed the door behind him on the way out. Those girls, he thought angrily, they get me talking and leave me to take it. I got to take all the trouble!

Once outside the classroom, it did not take him long to discover that the headmaster's office was empty. From the window he could see the men in the builders' yard on the far side of the council car park playing dodgem cars with their fork-lift trucks. Colin watched them veering in and out of the piles of bricks and drainpipes.

"Those girls!" he repeated out loud. "They better watch out when that bell goes."

When he got fed up of looking out of the window, he began to swing himself up and down the staircase by the wooden banisters. It was while he was leaping down the steps for the third time that he spotted the new notice. It stopped him in his tracks.

"I am hoping to run a school cricket team . . ."

When the bell went, Trinton Adams was the first out of the

8

music room. Miss Ringrose had forgotten that she was supposed to be keeping him behind after school, and he was intent on getting as far away as possible before she remembered.

Colin caught hold of him on the stairs.

"Let go," Trinton protested, "let go my arm. Miss'll kill me if she catch me, man."

"Look at this," Colin insisted. "Look at the notice, Trint."

So Trinton became the second of the boys to see the new notice.

There was still a huddle of boys around the notice ten minutes after school had ended.

"Hey, cricket! That'll be smart."

"See me bat. I knock it for six, all over the field."

"I'll believe that when I see it," Trinton said. "Anyway, we ain't even got a field, so how we supposed to run a cricket team?"

"We've got the yard."

"The yard? The school yard? How we supposed to play cricket in there with windows all around? You tell me that. Anyway, no one play real cricket on tarmac."

"Mr Bunting must have thought of all that, Trint, or else why would he put up this notice?"

The discussion continued so noisily that it eventually drew Mr Jackson, the deputy headmaster, from the staff room at the foot of the stairs. He stood holding his cup of tea, and coughed loudly. Gradually the boys fell silent and turned to face him.

"The bell went approximately twelve minutes ago, gentlemen," he said, consulting his wristwatch. "The

9

school rules state quite clearly that you must vacate the premises within fifteen minutes of the end of school, unless you are engaged in some authorized activity in the company of a member of staff."

"We're just looking at this notice."

"You've had plenty of time to read everything on that noticeboard. I suggest you now leave. I will expect you to be clear of the gates in . . . um . . . exactly two minutes."

Slowly, the boys walked down the staircase and past the deputy headmaster.

"Putting up bleeding notices," grumbled someone, "and us not allowed to study them."

"Stop!" said Mr Jackson. "Who said that?"

The boys turned to face him. None of them would speak. Most looked down at their feet, or concentrated on staring at a particular brick in the brown painted wall behind Mr Jackson. Suddenly Trinton and Colin looked at each other and broke into giggles.

"Right!" snapped Mr Jackson. "The rest of you may go. You two, Adams and Tremaine, stay behind."

When the rest of the boys had drifted silently away, Mr Jackson took a sip of his tea and looked down at Trinton and Colin.

"Now," he began, adopting his quiet, reasonable tone of voice, "I can't say for sure who it was who passed that remark as you were coming down the stairs, but I'd stake a month's salary that it was one of you two . . ."

"You'd lose it then," Trinton interrupted. "It wasn't us."

"Quiet!" Mr Jackson's voice rose considerably. "I've had too many complaints about your behaviour already: noisy, disruptive, lazy, rude and insolent. I won't have it! My staff have enough on their plates trying to educate you, without having to put up with your bad manners on top of their other difficulties."

Colin fought hard to stifle his laughter. He was thinking about Mr Jackson betting and losing his wages. Anyone could tell it was Froggy James who had spoken; you could pick his croaky voice out in a football crowd.

Trinton concentrated on the lettering on the staff room door, reading it over and over to himself: Staff Room – Please Knock and Wait. He did not interrupt again, but allowed the deputy headmaster to have his say.

". . . understand?" Mr Jackson concluded. "Don't let me hear any more complaints about you two, or you won't have time to look at notices after school. You'll be doing extra work for me, every night if necessary. Is that clear?"

Colin and Trinton mumbled a reply and turned to go.

"By the way," added Mr Jackson, as an afterthought, "why this sudden interest in Colorado Beetles?"

Nirmal Singh left school later than usual that night. In science, someone had knocked over his test tube full of chemicals when he was halfway through his experiment, and he had had to start again. He was still not sure whether it had been an accident or not, but the science teacher had insisted on him completing the practical. That was why he was almost half an hour late coming down the staircase past the noticeboard. His sharp eyes picked out the unfamiliar notice immediately.

Outside the gates, a gang of boys had gathered to wait for Colin and Trinton. They sat on the bench or leant against the wire netting fence. One or two practised tricks on their bicycles, pedalling along the road between the school and the car park.

"What did he do?" they asked as soon as Colin and Trinton appeared. "He give you a licking?"

"Nah," Colin replied. "Jackson don't do nothing but talk."

"Right," Trinton added. "Him just talk about beetles."

"Beetles?" the gang of boys shouted incredulously.

"Yeah, and you should've heard Trint," Colin took up the story. "Old Jackson says he'd bet his wages . . ."

The howls of laughter that greeted Colin's tale reached the ears of those teachers who were still drinking tea in the staff room.

"Haven't they got homes to go to?" asked Miss Ringrose, whose head was still aching from her music lesson with 4C.

"Yes," said Mr Jackson, "but in most cases there'll be no one there yet, so what's the point?"

"But it's so infuriating," continued Miss Ringrose. "They're so unwilling when they've got to be here, but as soon as we want them to go, they hang around till all hours. I've a good mind to have a word with the head about it."

"You'll have to catch him in first," chuckled Mr Jackson. "He's been out at one of his meetings all afternoon."

Nirmal hesitated on his way towards the school gates. These boys, West Indians and white boys, were no friends of his. None of them was in his class. They were mostly 4C boys, the ones who were always in trouble at school: Colin Tremaine and Trinton Adams, who had often made fun of his Sikh headdress, Alan James, the small white boy who everyone called Froggy, and Ross Marsh, the biggest boy in the school. Froggy James was the worst, Nirmal thought; he was always shouting and calling names when his big friends were about to protect him.

"Hey!" someone shouted, interrupting Nirmal's train of thought. "It's Singh."

Nirmal stopped at the gate. He smiled to disguise his misgivings as all the boys, including the cyclists, gathered round him.

"You been in trouble?" Trinton asked.

"Not likely," said Froggy James. "Singh doesn't get in trouble. He's a good boy, isn't he? Always does what he's told."

"What's he late for, then?" asked Ross Marsh.

"I had trouble with my practical in science," explained Nirmal, still smiling, "and I had to do it again."

"Don't he talk funny?" said Froggy, mimicking Nirmal's voice. All the boys laughed and tried out their own versions of an Asian accent.

"Please, I must go now," Nirmal said, attempting to pass by the gang.

"We'll come with you," said Trinton, winking at the others, "you know, look after you and that."

"There is no need. I'm going to meet my father at the bus garage."

"Does he wear a hanky on his head like you?" asked Froggy.

"No," said Nirmal, struggling to keep control of his voice, "he wears a full turban most of the time. Now I must go, please."

"I don't think so," said Froggy, standing right in Nirmal's path.

The rest of the boys fanned out into a circle round him and Froggy. Froggy was not very tough, certainly not as tough as Ross who was known as the best fighter in school, but with everyone around he had a chance to build up his reputation. Clearly he did not intend to waste it.

Fortunately for Nirmal, who did not want to fight, Mr Halligan, the science teacher, chose that moment to come out of the staff room and into the yard.

Trinton spotted him and gave the signal for the boys to disperse. In twos and threes, the boys made off up the street.

"See you, Singh," Froggy called over his shoulder as he scooted off up the street. "We'll see you another time."

"Let's go practise cricket," Colin suggested.

"Gary Sobers, man," said Trinton.

"*Sir* Gary Sobers," Colin corrected him. "He knock them all for six."

"We going to show Bunting how cricket got to be played – West Indies fashion."

A chorus of voices, white and black, shouted agreement. Nirmal, still standing at the gate, began to have second thoughts about attending the cricket practice.

An hour later the school yard was deserted and the buildings were empty except for the cleaners.

In a terraced house two streets away from the school Nirmal sat and did his homework while his father and two uncles drank tea and watched the television news. Every so often they asked him to explain a word or an item that they did not fully understand.

In the next street Froggy James was alone in a basement flat with his baby brother. He had washed him and dressed him in his pyjamas and now he was feeding him biscuits and milk before putting him to bed. In the background, a transistor radio played record requests for people driving home from work.

Out on the street, Trinton still stood at his newspaper stand on the corner between the gents' outfitters and the social security offices. He worked this corner every night, selling papers to regular customers and casual passers-by alike. He would fetch the stand from the back of the gents' outfitters, pick up the stack of papers dropped from the delivery van and return the money and unsold papers to the van driver at the end of his night's work. Two hours a night, five nights a week, selling the regular evening paper, followed by extra time on Saturday selling the sports edition: this was better paid and carried more prestige than an ordinary paper round. Trinton had inherited the patch from an elder cousin who had found other, more lucrative ways of making money. He was spending his evenings now humping speakers and record decks for Fast Eddie, who ran the best sound system in town. His newspaper stand, meanwhile, was in capable hands. Although Trinton was only thirteen, no one thought of trying to take money or papers from his stand.

2

On Tuesday, April 14th, Miss Ringrose came into the staff room after school, looking even more distraught than usual.

"The yard's full of fourth year boys," she complained to anyone who would listen. "They wouldn't budge when I told them to leave. They say they're waiting for Mr Bunting."

"That's right," said Mr Halligan who was already warming the pot for tea. "Haven't you heard? Our Frank's decided to turn Jubilee Street into an outpost of the MCC."

"Pardon?"

"Cricket, my dear," said Mr Halligan, miming a stroke with a bat. "It's Frank's pet scheme to bring the races together. He thinks he can teach these delightful fourth years

16

to play the game like English gentlemen."

Any further conversation was prevented by the emergence of Mr Bunting himself from the gents' cloakroom that adjoined the staff room. He was wearing white plimsolls, grey flannel trousers, a white shirt and his club cricket sweater with two coloured stripes around the neck. Under his arm he carried a brand new bat, spotless in its polythene wrapper.

"My God!" said Mr Halligan. "You really mean it, don't you?"

Mr Bunting, a young man in his first teaching job, nodded and strode through the staff room without a word.

"Here he is, here's sir," the boys shouted as Mr Bunting approached.

"Is this shirt all right? Only I haven't got a white one, but me mum found this cream one that me brother used to wear for work. It's got no buttons, though . . ."

"Gather round, boys," Mr Bunting shouted.

"Can I hold your bat, sir?"

"Hey, smart! Will we have bats like that?"

"I've only got black shoes, Mr Bunting."

"Quiet!" roared Mr Bunting. "Into the changing room now and get changed for the practice."

"But these shoes, Mr Bunting . . ."

"No more questions. In!"

Nineteen boys crowded into a hut that would only comfortably take half a dozen brooms and a bucket. The sixteen hooks on the wall were immediately snatched. The three boys left without hooks to hang their clothes on were, as Mr Bunting observed, Nirmal Singh and two other Asian boys.

"Sorry, but you lads will have to pile your clothes neatly

17

on the floor," said Mr Bunting. "Either that or share a peg with someone."

"No chance."

"They ain't sharing my peg."

Mr Bunting pretended not to hear. It was sometimes easier that way.

"Come on now," he said, clapping his hands. "Let's get out and make a start."

Once outside, he lined the boys up against a wall at the side of the yard. They stood alongside their own friends in a wide variety of clothing and footwear. In fact, the only boy who had a white shirt and white plimsolls was Nirmal Singh. Mr Bunting called him out in front of the other boys.

"Right," he said. "First things first. When I say white shirt and plimsolls, this is what I mean. This is what I expect you to wear for cricket, not multi-coloured shirts, James."

Froggy James made a defiant clicking noise with his tongue. Mr Bunting continued regardless.

"In order to play cricket properly, you have to be turned out in the right gear. If you look the part, you play that much better. Believe me, I've been playing this game for long enough to have learned that. Thank you, Nirmal. You can rejoin the others."

Colin muttered out loud. Nirmal did not hear the exact words, but he sensed the hostility. So did Mr Bunting.

"Have you got something to say, Tremaine?" he asked. "If so, I'm sure we'd all like to hear from you."

"All this white shirt and shoes stuff," Colin grumbled. "It's all right for him; he's already got them . . ."

"Yes," agreed Mr Bunting, "and I expect you to get them too."

18

"What if we can't?"

"What he's saying," interrupted Trinton, "is that most of us ain't got those things you just said, and he want to know . . . *we* want to know what you going to do if we can't get them."

"I can't get them," added Froggy. "Me mum says it's not worth getting special stuff just for cricket when I'm leaving this school in the summer. I've only got these black shoes, and if they won't do, it's just too bad."

"Right!" said Trinton. "That goes for me too."

All eyes were on Mr Bunting.

"I see," he said, thinking fast. "For today's practice I am prepared to relax the rules about clothing. However, before the next practice, I will want to see a real effort to kit yourselves out properly. If you genuinely have problems, come and see me, and I'll see what we can do to help. Is that understood?"

The practice began. Mr Bunting produced a canvas bag of cricket equipment. From it he took half a dozen bats, mostly old and held together with tape. The blades were cracked and dirty, and the handles had long since lost their rubber grips.

"Is this all the bats we got?" complained Trinton. "These are rubbish."

"We have two or three newer bats," Mr Bunting told him, "but they're too expensive to use for practices in the yard. I'm saving them for matches. Now put those bats down until I tell you to pick them up."

From the bag he took an assortment of worn-out tennis balls and a block of chalk.

"That's for the wickets, isn't it?" Froggy said, grabbing

the chalk. "We usually draw them on the wall over here. I'll do it."

"No you won't!" Mr Bunting shouted, his patience finally running out. "Let's get one thing straight right from the start. You're here to do what you're told. Put that chalk down or go home now."

Froggy did not like being shouted at; it made him feel small. He threw down the block of chalk and set off home.

"Bloody silly practice I call this anyway," he croaked over his shoulder. Some of the boys sniggered.

"Anyone else want to join him?" Mr Bunting asked. "Marsh? Adams? If you can't take this seriously, go now before we start."

The boys said nothing but waited impatiently, shifting their weight from one foot to the other. This practice was taking a long time to get started. Mr Bunting looked down at the scrap of paper on which he had planned the way the practice would go. 'Warm-up activity', it read, 'fielding practice'. He would have to scrub that and go straight into the main activity – 'basic batting strokes'.

The boys all looked down at the shapes Mr Bunting had drawn on the playground with the chalk. What was it all about?

"I'll demonstrate," said Mr Bunting. "These two shapes are where you put your feet. See? Not too far apart, just enough for a comfortable stance. Now, holding your bat . . ."

Mr Bunting took his own bat out of its polythene wrapper.

". . . firmly but not too lightly, get ready to play the ball."

He looked round at the watching group. Who could he rely on to obey his instructions?

"Nirmal Singh," he decided, "get a couple of balls and

serve them to me from about five yards away."

"Serve them?" Nirmal asked, bewildered.

"Yeah, on a plate, I think he means," suggested Trinton.

"Just toss them underarm so that they bounce in the circle I've drawn in front of my feet," explained Mr Bunting.

"'Course you sure to get balls like that in a match," said Trinton scornfully. "Underarm and just where you can hit them!"

"You others," continued Mr Bunting, ignoring Trinton's remarks, "act as fielders. Spread out there, on Nirmal's left. That's what we call the offside of the field."

"Didn't know you had offside in cricket," said Colin, talking, as usual, directly into Trinton's right ear. "Hey, Trint, I said . . ."

"Heard you, boy," said Trinton. "Leave the jokes to me. I better at telling them than you."

Nirmal tossed the ball very slowly into the circle. In his eagerness, Mr Bunting pushed his foot and bat forward too early. The ball popped up into the hands of Ross Marsh who clutched it to his chest.

"Out!" said Colin.

"Next batter," added Trinton, snapping his fingers.

"That's how not to play the stroke," explained Mr Bunting.

"You don't say!" exclaimed Trinton.

"Again, please, Nirmal. But throw it a little harder this time."

Nirmal did. Mr Bunting timed his stroke correctly this time and pushed the ball firmly along the ground to a fielder who stopped the ball with his foot.

"There," said Mr Bunting, "you see? To drive the ball safely along the ground, you need to put your foot forward to where the ball bounces and play the stroke with the face of the bat pointing downwards so that you hit the ball into the ground. Just once more, please, Nirmal."

Again Mr Bunting pushed the ball firmly along the ground to Ross. Trinton laughed.

"No runs for that shot," he said.

"Right, Adams," said Mr Bunting, "you've had plenty to say for yourself. Now let's see what you can do."

Trinton, though, shook his head and pushed Colin forward.

"You want a batter?" he said. "Colin's your man. Me – I'm a bowler myself, you know, plenty of speed and that, but Colin's the one to show you about batting."

"All right then, Tremaine. You'll do just as well," said Mr Bunting. "Put your feet on those marks."

Colin tried, but his feet would not settle in the chalk marks.

"Nah!" he said. "Can't get comfortable like that."

He spread his feet wide apart and gripped the bat firmly.

"Now, remember," Mr Bunting reminded him. "I want to see you hit the ball into the ground so that there's no danger of your being caught."

"Come on, Singh. Send one down."

The fielders and Mr Bunting watched. Nirmal lobbed the ball into the circle. Colin wound the bat up round his shoulders and smacked the ball high into the air over the bike sheds.

The fielders laughed and cheered. Trinton snapped his fingers.

"Six runs, I think," he called out.

Colin simply leant on his bat and beamed as Mr Bunting wondered what to do next.

3

"Stand still!" called out Mr Jackson in Monday morning assembly. "And stop that coughing and shuffling!"

The children of Jubilee Street School were crowded into the main hall which had not been designed to hold such numbers. The younger children stood at the front of the hall in straight lines, but the older ones huddled together at the back, defying the attempts of their teachers to get them to stand in line.

"Tremaine!" shouted Mr Jackson. "Are you eating, boy?"

"No," said Colin who was leaning against a radiator at the very back of the hall.

"Are you sure?"

"Yes," said Colin, tucking a wad of chewing gum under his tongue and opening his mouth wide to prove his point. All the children in the hall turned round to look at him, which made him open his mouth even wider and hang his tongue even further over his bottom lip. An outbreak of laughter, begun by Trinton, quickly spread round the hall.

"That will do!" Mr Jackson shouted.

". . . for ever and ever, amen."

"Right, look up, please," the headmaster said as the mumbled prayer came to an end. "Just one or two brief notices this morning."

By the radiator at the back of the hall, someone broke wind. Mr Jackson stepped out smartly from his position at the side of the hall to investigate. He stared into a sea of faces, in the midst of which were Colin's and Trinton's, grinning hugely at each other.

"Tremaine and Adams," Mr Jackson said, "see me after assembly."

"Wasn't me," protested Trinton.

"Nor me," added Colin.

"We'll discuss that later. Now keep quiet."

All eyes turned back to the headmaster who was sorting out a handful of notices.

"Yes. Now, pay attention," he said, finally locating the first notice. "Ah . . . the chess club wishes you all to know that it is again meeting regularly in Room Four on Monday lunchtimes. If you're interested, see Nirmal Singh for further details."

"Huh!" grunted Trinton, drawing a stare from Mr Jackson.

"And Miss Ringrose," continued the headmaster, "has asked me to remind you all that there are still places waiting to be filled in the school choir. In particular, she is short of boys' voices. Now then, you lads, I bet you're quite happy to go along to the football ground in winter and sing your hearts out there. Well, singing in a choir is much the same thing, you know. It's a chance to enjoy yourself making a noise."

Laughter spread around the hall, particularly towards the back.

"Quiet!" shouted Mr Jackson. "Quiet while the headmaster's speaking."

"Ah, thank you," continued the head. "Still, that proves my point. You enjoy making a noise, so why not do it constructively by joining the choir?"

"They sing such crappy songs, that's why," whispered Trinton, under his breath.

Unfortunately, it was not far enough under; Mr Jackson sidled over and spoke to him out of the side of his mouth.

"I'll see to you after assembly."

"And finally," announced the headmaster, "Mr Bunting tells me that the cricket team practices are going well. The next one is tomorrow night after school, and the fixture list for the term is to be posted on the main noticeboard at the head of the stairs. I'm looking forward to more good reports on the progress of the team, and I hope you remember to play the game in the proper spirit."

The headmaster smiled out over the rows and rows of faces. None smiled back at him.

"Now, there's just one more thing I'd like to say," he began again, raising his voice over a fresh outbreak of coughing and foot shuffling. "We had to call the police in again last week, I'm afraid; there was another break-in at the school. Fortunately, no serious damage was done this time. But the culprits did make a hell of a mess of the domestic science room. That's one reason why I want these people caught: they make too much unnecessary work for the cleaning and caretaking staff."

Mr Jackson looked at all the faces at the back of the hall; he was convinced that the culprits were boys from within the school.

"If you know anything," continued the headmaster, "anything at all about this or any of the other break-ins, come and tell me. I know that sounds like telling tales, but, in this case, it's not. This is your school, and you must help us to look after it."

Every face was blank. There was no sign of guilt, no clue at all for Mr Jackson to follow up.

Yet again Trinton and Colin stood side by side in front of Mr Jackson.

"I'm not going to waste words on you two," Mr Jackson began. "We've enough to worry about with these break-ins, without having to put up with your uncivilized behaviour."

Trinton adopted his usual practice of examining the wall behind the deputy head's shoulder. It was covered with paintings and collages. There was one sheet of paper covered in tin cans, bottle tops, bits of string and sacking, all heavily coated with red gloss paint. 'Moon Base', it was called.

"You both fancy yourselves as cricketers, I hear," the deputy head continued. "Is that so?"

Colin shrugged. Trinton smiled, still avoiding Mr Jackson's eyes.

"And you don't have much time for singing and the activities of the school choir? Well?"

"It's all right," Colin said. "Just don't want to join the choir, that's all. I ain't much good at singing."

"And you, Adams?"

"No thanks," said Trinton. "Miss Ringrose says my voice is flat. She don't even like me singing in music lessons."

"In that case," said Mr Jackson, speaking very quietly and precisely, "perhaps you could both do with some singing practice after school?"

"We got cricket practices after school," said Trinton.

"Not unless your behaviour improves, you haven't," smiled Mr Jackson. "You'll be doing some singing practice for me instead of cricket practice. If I have one more complaint about your behaviour in school, you'll be showing me what sweet voices you have."

"That's not fair!" protested Colin.

"Fair?" replied Mr Jackson. "Was it fair of you to continually interrupt our assembly? Was it fair of you to make foul odours during an act of worship?"

Colin looked puzzled by this last remark, but Trinton immediately understood the nature of the accusation.

"We told you that wasn't us."

"Yeah," Colin added, catching on. "We told you before."

"And I don't choose to believe you, either of you. I've heard too many lies from you in the past."

"Suit yourself," said Trinton. "But we telling you the gospel truth."

"That's enough!" snapped Mr Jackson. "I've given you fair warning: one more complaint from any member of staff and I'll be keeping you in tomorrow night. Is that clear?"

Neither boy spoke.

"Is that clear?" Mr Jackson repeated.

"Wasn't us," mumbled Colin.

"I don't want to hear about it," said Mr Jackson. "You know very well that you've done enough to deserve a whole month of punishments. Now go to your classes and don't let me hear any more complaints about you."

The two boys went, but slowly enough to show that they still felt that an injustice had been committed.

The list of fixtures duly appeared.

Jubilee Street Middle School Under Thirteen
Cricket Team

All matches will be played away since the school has not got proper facilities.

June 4   Jubilee Street Middle School v Lawton Road Middle School (away)

June 11 Jubilee Street Middle School v Abbeyfields Middle School (away)

June 26 Jubilee Street Middle School v Grove Lane Middle School (away)

July 4   Jubilee Street Middle School v Priory School (away)

F. R. Bunting

". . . the Priory School? Where's that?" someone asked.

"Never heard of it," shrugged Froggy James. "It ain't round here."

"It is," said Nirmal Singh, looking over the shoulders of

the boys who were crowding round the noticeboard. Froggy turned round to stare at Nirmal.

"Who asked you?" he sneered.

The other boys ignored Froggy and, instead, asked Nirmal:

"Where is it, then, Singh? This Priory School?"

"It is a private school," he told them, "on the other side of town. The boys all wear grey blazers with a red badge."

"Oh yeah, I've seen them on the buses sometimes."

"Are they the ones that have all those fields by the river?" another boy asked.

"Yes, I think so," said Nirmal. "They seem to have a lot of good facilities at that school."

He was part of the group now, edging closer to the noticeboard.

"How come you know so much about it?" asked Froggy, shouldering his way back to the centre of attention.

"We played there last term," said Nirmal.

"Who?"

"The chess club. They have very good players at the Priory School: the best in the district."

"Huh!" said Froggy scornfully. As usual his voice came out as a high-pitched croak. "That's at chess, but I bet we can mash them at cricket. You wait and see."

"I thought you had given up cricket at the first practice," said Nirmal.

The scowl on Froggy's face made Nirmal wish that he had kept his thoughts to himself.

At lunchtime the classrooms emptied. Playground supervisors, housewives from the neighbourhood, patrolled the school yard while all the teachers except one stayed behind the firmly closed staff room door. Colin and Trinton stood together outside that very door. They leant against the wall and talked quietly and gloomily.

"Some teachers," muttered Colin, "you can't have no fun with them."

"Uh-huh," Trinton grunted in agreement.

"I mean," continued Colin, "we was only having a bit of a laugh, and we didn't do the girls no harm."

"Sure," said Trinton. "And another thing, that playground woman shouldn't have spoken to us the way she did but you try telling Halligan that."

"You did try," Colin reminded him, "but it only made him madder than ever."

Both boys fell silent. Colin stared down at his feet, and tried to place them like Mr Bunting had told him to at batting practice. It still did not feel right like that. He would fall over if he tried to hit the ball with his feet so close together. The memory of that first practice made him smile suddenly. Trinton looked across at him.

"What you laughing at?" he asked.

"See me hit that six!" Colin chuckled. "Then Bunting bet me I couldn't do it with him bowling properly."

"So? You didn't hit his ball. You missed it."

"Only because I didn't want to lose another ball," said Colin. "They never found that first one, you know."

"Yes, but you hear Bunting?" interrupted Trinton. "He say I make a good opening bowler. Fast bowler, man!"

"I hit the sixes and you hit the wickets," said Colin. "We show them, West Indies style!"

For a moment both boys beamed. Then, together, they remembered Mr Jackson's threat to keep them in at the time of the cricket practice.

"Perhaps he let us off this time?" Colin suggested hopefully.

"Not a chance," said Trinton with a greater grasp of reality. "He come past and see us here, or else Halligan tell him how he catch us in the girls' toilet. He got us for sure this time."

At that precise moment their fate was being discussed behind the staff room door.

"Whooping like Zulus," Mr Halligan explained, "and putting the fear of God into the poor girls."

"You mean they were right inside the toilets?" asked Miss Ringrose.

"Right inside," confirmed Mr Halligan. "I heard those delightful war cries that we've all come to associate with Adams and Tremaine, and I had to get Mrs Whitworth to turf them out. They were, needless to say, very abusive to her in the process."

"You mean they swore at her?" asked Mr Jackson.

"More than once, by her account," replied Mr Halligan. "She intends to speak to the head about it."

"That just about puts the cap on it," said Mr Jackson.

"Of course, Adams tried to talk his way out of it," Mr Halligan continued. "He said that Mrs Whitworth had provoked them into swearing back at her, and got quite abusive to me when I refused to listen."

Mr Jackson shook his head and turned to Mr Bunting, who was marking books at a work table.

"Frank," he said, "are those two characters essential members of your . . . er . . . cricket team by any chance?"

"Who? Colin Tremaine and Trinton Adams?"

"Who else?"

Mr Bunting looked up from his books. He pondered for a moment.

"Yes," he decided. "They're rather raw, of course, but they have plenty of enthusiasm and lots of natural talent. I expect them both to be part of the team."

"In that case," announced Mr Jackson, "I think you may have to revise your plans. I don't think there's been a single school day this year that those two haven't been referred to me for some misdemeanour or other, and I have finally had enough. Swearing at Mrs Whitworth is the last straw. If they refuse to abide by the rules of a civilized school community, I see no reason why they should benefit from the extra activities we provide. Consequently I have no intention of letting either Adams or Tremaine join in any out-of-school activities until their behaviour shows a marked improvement."

Then, he sank back into his chair and closed his eyes.

Nirmal stood outside the door, trying to avoid the two pairs of staring eyes. He hesitated, then tapped nervously on the door.

"They won't answer, Singh," Trinton told him.

"Mr Halligan told me to come," said Nirmal. "He said he would open Room Four for the chess club meeting."

"Oh yeah, chess club," Trinton nodded. Then, changing the subject, he added, "I tell you what, Singh."

"What?"

"I hear that Froggy James is looking for you."

Trinton and Colin laughed loud enough to bring Mr Halligan out of the staff room.

"Now then," he said. "What's all this noise about?"

Colin and Trinton said nothing. Mr Halligan turned directly to Nirmal with a questioning look in his eyes.

"Well?" he asked.

"It . . . it was nothing," said Nirmal. "I was just asking Trinton if he had seen you and he told me he thought you were in the staff room."

"Oh yes?"

"Yes, sir," said Nirmal. "That is all it was."

"And you, Adams?" asked Mr Halligan. "Do you agree with that version of events?"

"Something like that, yeah," Trinton agreed, but he did not look at either Mr Halligan or Nirmal.

4

In the music room, Mr Jackson sat at the piano. Trinton and Colin stood facing him, each holding a hymn book.

"Now," said Mr Jackson, "let's try number six hundred and fifty-four. Six-five-four, Tremaine, do try to find it without any help from Adams. And, remember, I want to hear a joyful noise from you both. After three . . ."

Unwillingly Colin and Trinton poured out the words, keeping up as best they could with Mr Jackson's heavy-handed piano playing.

> "*The King of love my shepherd is*
> *Whose goodness faileth never;*

I nothing lack if I am his
And he is mine for ever . . ."

In the gaps between the verses, they could hear the sounds of cricket practice in the yard outside: ball against bat, the shouts of the fielders, and Mr Bunting issuing instructions and words of encouragement.

". . . And so through all the length of days
Thy goodness faileth never;
Good Shepherd, may I sing thy praise
Within thy house for ever."

Later that same evening Trinton stood at his street corner while Colin was nearby, sitting on his bike which was propped up against the kerb.

"I'd like to take you, Col," Trinton was saying, juggling with handfuls of coin from his money tray, "but you know Eddie. Fast Eddie don't like a lot of kids hanging round his place."

"Yeah, so you say."

"That's how he is, Col. He only let me in the place because Johnny's doing work for him, wiring up his new speaker boxes; plenty bass, man! I help Johnny, so Eddie let me go along with him. Maybe he let us play some of his records. He got all the best sounds, you know, Fast Eddie."

"Yeah," said Colin, kicking his pedals. "I wonder if Bunting's picked the cricket team now?"

"He said he was going to," said Trinton, his mind still on Eddie's records and the prospect of helping his cousin Johnny that night.

"Anyway, we won't be in it, not if he done it like he said

and only pick from the people who went to practice today."

"It's all Jackson's fault," complained Colin, "picking on us for no good reason."

"Yeah, too bad," Trinton agreed, stopping to serve a couple of regular customers. As he handed over their change, he became aware of someone standing alongside him.

"Hello, Trint," said a voice. "What're you doing?"

The voice was immediately recognizable: Froggy James!

"What's it look like, Frog?" Trinton replied. "You think I standing here for the good of my health? I'm selling papers, boy, just like every night. Anyway, what *you* doing? Why ain't you back home with your kid brother?"

"He's been took to my aunty's," explained Froggy. "My mum's changed her hours at the pub, so that my aunty can look after our Shane at nights. What're you doing then, when you've finished your papers? Want to come round with me?"

"Where to?" asked Trinton. "You going to bust in again tonight?"

"No," said Froggy, "I got some other business to see to."

"I reckon anyone'd be crazy to go in tonight," said Colin. "It ain't long since we went in last time. They be on the lookout for someone busting in."

"I don't see that," said Trinton. "The police ain't that worried about some school being bust into. What harm we done?"

"Yeah, but you see Jackson, man, in assembly the other morning," Colin asked, "when the head was talking about it? He kept looking straight at us lot, you know."

"That's nothing," said Trinton. "There's nothing they can pin on us. We didn't leave no prints or nothing. I bet they don't even know how we got in. I leave that window clean, man: clean as a whistle like Johnny show me. Anyway," he added, looking in Froggy's direction, "what other business you got in mind?"

"Me and Ross is going round to Singh's," said Froggy. "I've still got to see to him, for what he said this morning. I'm going round his house."

"Oh, sure," said Trinton. "Sure, I can just see you going in his front door, past his old man . . ."

"His dad's at work," interrupted Froggy. "I just seen him going down the bus garage."

"So?" asked Trinton. "You still got to get past his front door to see to him."

Colin kicked his bike pedals and grinned. He and Trinton both knew that Froggy would do nothing on his own. Winking at Trinton, he said to Froggy: "I reckon Singh could take you, Frog. He ain't so soft, you know."

Froggy swore in reply, raising laughter from Colin and Trinton. This made Froggy bluster even more.

"I don't need you. I don't need anyone to take Singh. You saw how scared he was the other night."

"Yeah," agreed Trinton. "When we was all there. How you going to make out on your own, though?"

"I won't be on my own," said Froggy. "I told you, I'm going for Ross. Are you two coming or not?"

"Nah," said Trinton. "I got better things to do, man. I'm going round to Eddie's when I've finished the papers."

"Eddie's?" asked Froggy. "Who's he?"

"You wouldn't know him," said Trinton, attending to his dwindling pile of papers. "He's one of our people."

Froggy turned instead to Colin.

"What about you? You coming?"

Colin leant against his handlebars. Turning to Trinton, he raised his eyebrows questioningly. Trinton, though, shrugged.

"You know how it is, Col. I'd take you if I could, but Eddie's a bit strict about who he has in his place."

Colin stamped down on the pedals and began to cycle away down the side road.

"I'm fed up with hanging round anyway," he called out. "See you tomorrow."

Froggy stood and watched him go while Trinton leant nonchalantly against his paper stand.

"See you, Froggy," he said.

"What?"

Froggy was confused by the sudden turn of events.

"See you, I said," Trinton repeated. "If you're planning to give Singh a licking, you better get round there before it's time for bed."

"Right," said Froggy, rediscovering his determination. "You wait till tomorrow. You'll all see Singh then to see what I done to him – that is, if he dares to come to school after I see to him."

Trinton chuckled as he watched Froggy dodging through the traffic to cross the main road, his shirt tail flapping over the seat of his ragged jeans as he scooted between a bus and a furniture van.

Nirmal was alone in the house when he heard the clatter at the front door. Immediately his heart began to pound. Being alone in the house was something he was still not used to, even though it was now more than a month since his mother had returned to the Punjab with his two sisters. On evenings such as this, when his father was on late shift and his uncles did not come to drink tea, he would turn on the television loud, whether he wanted to watch it or not, to drown out all the noises that gave him cause for concern.

Now he listened hard, hoping not to hear. But there it was again: a rattling, banging noise against the front door. It was not the sound of a friend knocking to gain admittance. It sounded angry, like someone kicking the wooden panels.

Nirmal did not go to answer the door. Instead he crept up the stairs and into the front bedroom. Slowly he edged close to the window to look down into the street. It was still light enough to see that the street was empty of passers-by. Indeed there was no one at all outside his door. He waited and kept watch.

Suddenly, from behind a wall on the other side of the street, two figures appeared. It was Froggy James and Ross Marsh.

As Nirmal watched, Froggy hurled a handful of pebbles at the door: his door. The clattering echoed through the empty house. What to do? If he stayed upstairs and kept quiet, they would not see him. Perhaps Froggy would get tired of throwing stones and go away? Perhaps a neighbour would see him and send him away? Perhaps, though, he would grow bolder and throw at the windows? There was little enough money in the house as it was; air fares to India for his mother and sisters had taken a large slice of his father's savings. They could not afford to pay for damage to the house. No. Nirmal knew what he would have to do. He would have to go out and face Froggy and Ross.

Making sure he had a door key in his pocket, Nirmal opened the front door slowly. Froggy was about to release another handful of stones.

"Don't throw stones at our door!" Nirmal called out. "If you want someone here, knock on the door like everyone else."

39

Froggy drew back his arm, but seeing Nirmal still stand in the doorway, he simply lobbed the stones into the road.

"You've come out then," he said. "It's about time."

"What do you want?"

"I want you," said Froggy, pointing across the street at Nirmal. He looked for all the world like some gunslinger from the Wild West with his thumbs hooked under the belt of his jeans. Ross, Nirmal noticed, did nothing. He just sat on the wall with his arms folded.

"What do you want me for?" said Nirmal, surprised to find that his voice came out sounding calm and even.

"You know what for," Froggy spat out. "What you said at school this morning, by the noticeboard."

Nirmal stood his ground.

"I only said I thought you'd given up going to cricket practices."

"Oh yes?" said Froggy, advancing across the road. "And I suppose you think that you're great at cricket, but you're not, you know. I heard that Colin hit your bowling over the bike sheds."

"What has that to do with it?" asked Nirmal.

"You think you're good," sneered Froggy, "just because you get good marks and play chess and all that. Well, the teachers might think you're something special, but we don't, do we, Ross?"

Ross was still sitting on the wall on the far side of the road. Froggy waited for him to catch up before advancing even closer towards Nirmal's front door.

"All I said was that I thought you did not want to play cricket," Nirmal repeated.

"Stop saying that!" Froggy shouted. "Over and over again, you keep saying the same thing. I'm getting fed up with it, Singh."

Slowly but surely it dawned on Nirmal that Froggy was talking too much. If he had really wanted to cause trouble he would have started before now. This thought gave Nirmal confidence.

"I don't want to fight," he told Froggy. "I have no reason to fight with you."

"He's scared," said Froggy, turning to Ross. "That's what he means. He's scared, isn't he, Ross?"

"No," said Nirmal. "I have no quarrel with Ross, but if *you* must fight, I'll fight you back. If you're just going to talk nonsense, though, I'm going back inside."

"Come on, Ross," said Froggy, clenching his fists and raising his arms, "we can have him, no trouble."

Nirmal remained in the doorway and watched apprehensively as Froggy edged closer forward.

Just at that moment the Singhs' next door neighbour, an old lady with a passion for bingo, came out of her house on her way to the Tuesday night Tombola at the local community centre.

"Hello, love," she said to Nirmal. "On your own again, are you?"

Nirmal nodded politely and was relieved to see Froggy's arms fall to his sides and his fists unclench. Not knowing what else to do, Froggy turned away and began to kick a cigarette packet along the pavement.

"See you some other time, Singh," he called over his shoulder.

Ross chuckled and followed Froggy.

"Are they friends of yours?" asked Nirmal's neighbour.

"They go to my school," replied Nirmal.

The old lady shook her head.

"That little one, I know his mother," she said. "At least, I see her about the streets a lot. I shouldn't have anything to do with him if I were you, love. He's only likely to lead you into bad ways."

Nirmal said nothing; he simply continued to nod and smile politely. The old lady prepared to go on her way but, as an afterthought, she turned to speak again just as Nirmal was about to retreat indoors.

"You were late home from school tonight, weren't you? You get in much earlier as a rule."

"Yes," said Nirmal. "We had a practice for the cricket team."

"I see," said the old lady. "You're in the cricket team, are you?"

"I hope to be," said Nirmal, trying to sound modest. "Mr Bunting – he's our cricket teacher – thinks I have a good chance if I can improve my bowling."

"Does he? That's very good, isn't it? Still, your people are often good at cricket, aren't they? At least, they seem to be from what I see in the paper, not that I know much about it myself."

With a last wave she turned and was on her way. Nirmal returned indoors and closed the door behind him, hoping that he had seen the last of Froggy James for that night at least.

Colin cycled slowly up and down Jubilee Street.

After leaving Trinton and Froggy at the street corner earlier in the evening, he had gone home, but there had been nothing for him to do there. His dad was doing some more painting and decorating, piling up the furniture and covering everything with sheets of newspaper. There was nowhere Colin could sit to get comfortable.

His mother would not let him have the television on either,

because his big sister Marcia was doing her homework. Marcia was at Upper School and was preparing for her exams.

"Exams got to come before television in this house, Colin," his mother said. "Marcia wants to get on well in these examinations. It's important to her."

Marcia looked up from her books.

"What about you, little brother?" she asked. "Haven't you got any homework tonight?"

"No," Colin grunted. "They didn't give us none today."

"*Any*," said Marcia. "They didn't give us *any* – that's what you should say. Huh! It seems to me that things have changed since I was at Jubilee Street, more ways than one. There always used to be plenty of work handed out when I was there; Sylvie, too."

"I remember that," said Mrs Tremaine. "Both my girls always had plenty time for their books. Pity you don't do the same, Colin."

For once, his father intervened on his behalf.

"Leave him be, you women. Lord, the boy told you he don't have no work tonight, and he know better than to tell lies, don't you, boy . . ."

Colin, seeing the strength of his father's arms and the width of his leather belt, nodded silently.

"Anyway," his father added, "Colin ain't one for book learning. I expect he do better at practical things. You wait till he get the chance to do woodwork and stuff."

"Correct me if I'm wrong," said Marcia, "but boys in the fourth year at Jubilee Street *do* do woodwork."

"That a fact?" said Colin's father. "Lord, woman, don't your daughter sound more like a grown woman every day . . ."

So Colin had gone back out on his bike, looking for

43

Trinton. Trinton, though, had finished his papers by this time and had gone. It was no use looking for him. Colin knew quite well where he would be by now. There had to be someone around that he could have some fun with: even Froggy would do. So Colin cycled slowly up and down the streets round school, looking for someone, looking for anyone; anyone would do.

5

When he saw the panda cars parked outside the main gates of the school, Trinton forgot all about looking for Froggy to find out what had happened at Nirmal Singh's house.

"Hey, Colin," he called out when he bumped into his friend in the yard, "there's police all over the place. What's happening?"

"Don't know," shrugged Colin. "They been in a long time, talking to Jackson and them."

"Let's go look," suggested Trinton, pulling Colin with him up the stairs to the hall. They got just a glimpse of the turmoil in one of the rooms off the hall – the music room – before Mr Halligan turned them away and sent them back out to the playground.

"I have a list of names here, headmaster," said Mr Bunting as the head came out of his office before school. "It's the team for our first cricket fixture . . ."

"Not now, if you please, Mr Bunting," said the headmaster, who was clearly in an agitated state. "I'm far too busy at the moment. We've had another break-in, you see . . ."

In the staff room, Mr Jackson took charge.

"Your classes," he told the assembled staff, "will report to you for registration in the main hall. The head has the police in now, and they will begin an investigation of the incident immediately."

"What exactly is the damage this time?" asked Mr Halligan. "Has much been stolen?"

"I don't think there's much missing," said Mr Jackson, shaking his head, "but the damage is extensive, I'm afraid. Many of the store cupboards have been emptied out completely, bottles of ink, tubes of glue and so on tipped all over the furniture. That's only superficial damage, though. The worst of it is that the little fiends left the taps running in the upstairs lavatory and flooded the whole area. It's left some of the rooms in a very bad way; the downstairs rooms have suffered most. Some of the ceiling plaster is down and many of the wall coverings are totally ruined."

"Any clue as to who did it?" asked Mr Halligan.

"Nothing yet," said Mr Jackson. "The police have not yet checked all the rooms, so I would ask you to keep quiet about all of this until further notice."

"See that?" said Trinton, once they were readmitted to the main hall.

"Someone turned that room over, all the desks and everything. Man, they made a real mess."

"Yes," said Colin without enthusiasm.

"Hope they wrecked that piano," said Trinton. "Could save us a lot of stupid singing if they have."

"The police are in, Trint," Colin pointed out. "You wait and see. They'll come ask us all about it: where we were, what we know and all that. You wait and see!"

"Man, they can question me all day. There was plenty people saw me at Eddie's last night. They can't say nothing about me breaking in the school."

"That don't matter one bit," said Colin. "They'll question us anyway. You wait and see."

"So what?" puzzled Trinton. "What's got into you, Col?"

They were outside the door of their own classroom, which had not been damaged in the break-in. Inside it, they could hear their class teacher calling the register.

"Come on," said Trinton. "We better go in now."

Colin slumped against the wall.

"Not yet," he said. "Listen, Trint. Do me a favour, will you?"

"Yeah, sure. Come on in and tell me all about it."

"No," said Colin. "Out here. I got to talk to you out here where no one listening to us."

"All right," said Trinton. "They can wait. Anyway, I hear we aren't having ordinary classes today. What is it you want from me?"

"Trint, if anyone ask, tell them I was with you at Fast Eddie's last night, will you? Just say that if they ask about me."

"Why?" asked Trinton. "Why you want me to alibi you? You didn't do nothing here, did you?"

"'Course not, Trint, but I was out by myself all night after I left you and Froggy. I didn't go home till late, not until my dad had finished his decorating."

"That's no account, man," said Trinton. "You didn't do any of this, so what you got to worry about?"

"I was out by myself," Colin repeated. "If I tell them that, they'll just keep picking on me, asking me over and over. I had all that before, you know the sort of thing. You know what it's like as well as me. It just make things easier, Trint, if I can say I was with you, helping Johnny round at Eddie's place. Only thing, though, if I say that, you got to back me up, Trint."

Trinton was still considering this request when the classroom door opened and their teacher poked his head out.

"Would you two gentlemen care to join us?" he asked. "Or do you intend to stay out here all day?"

Detective Sergeant Grundy cleared the desk in the medical room.

"I prefer a clear desk," he explained to the headmaster. "The less there is to distract them, the more chance I get to look into their eyes and simply wait. You'd be surprised how much you can turn up just by doing that."

"You're sure, are you, that this is . . . ah . . . an inside job?" asked the headmaster.

Detective Sergeant Grundy shrugged and arranged the chairs precisely on either side of the desk.

"You've seen for yourself," he said. "Nothing missing except a handful of balls and a cricket bat from the games cupboard. In my book, it's got to be kids. Of course, it doesn't have to be your kids, but, you never know, they hear a lot, don't they, on the grapevine, like . . . Anyway, it gives us somewhere to start. I had a word earlier with your deputy, Mr . . . er . . . what's his name?"

"Jackson, Mr Jackson."

"That's right. Your Mr Jackson gave me some names of lads that he thought I ought to see."

Detective Sergeant Grundy handed over a sheet of school notepaper, on which Mr Jackson had printed a brief list of names. Prominent on the list were the names: Adams T. and Tremaine C.

The headmaster scratched his head and tugged at his ear lobe.

"I can't give you a great deal of help, I'm afraid," he said. "You see, Mr Jackson has rather more day-to-day contact with these boys than I do. He keeps his ear very close to the ground as far as this sort of thing is concerned. I do know these two, though . . ."

He pointed out two names on the list as he handed it back to Detective Sergeant Grundy: Adams T. and Tremaine C.

". . . two of our West Indian fraternity, Colin Tremaine and . . . ah . . . Trinton, yes, Trinton Adams. They're very lively boys, I believe, and many of my staff seem to find them rather a handful in the classroom environment, but, beyond that, I can't really say. Perhaps you ought to meet them for yourself?"

Detective Sergeant Grundy had already made a mark next to the two names.

"I think I will," he said.

*

"Just take it easy, Col, that's all you got to do."

Trinton and Colin were together in the boys' toilets. Colin sat on the edge of a wash basin while Trinton combed his hair and examined his face in the cracked mirror.

"Yeah, but what did you say, Trint?" Colin asked nervously.

"I just answered the man's questions . . . No sweat."

Trinton bared his teeth to the mirror and picked at them with the end of his comb. Meanwhile, Colin kicked at the pipes under the basin with his heels.

"You go in there, Col," Trinton told him. "Grundy's sitting behind the desk. The head's in there, too, but he just sits and watches. Grundy asks all the questions. He leans right across the desk and stares at you, but all you got to do is stare right back at him. He soon gets tired of playing the big interrogator."

"You tell him you were at Eddie's?" Colin asked, trying to get back to the point.

"Sure," said Trinton, "when he asked me. But he was asking a lot more questions than that. Did I have a grudge against the school, against any of the teachers, all that sort of thing. I tell him, man: sure I do. Lots of teachers on my back, picking on me and so on."

"What he say to that?" asked Colin.

Trinton laughed aloud.

"Wanted to know what I do about it. I tell him straight: they pick on me, I pick on them. They get on my back, I get on theirs. Simple as that. Man, you should have seen their faces."

"So it's all right for me to say I was with you at Eddie's last night?" Colin asked, still in need of reassurance.

Trinton stopped attending to his face and hair and turned to look his friend in the face.

"You sure you don't know nothing about this stuff?" he asked directly.

Colin's head slumped against his chest.

"I bust in here last night," he admitted. "Don't say nothing, but I come in through that window, the way you showed me."

"On your own?" Trinton asked.

"Yeah," said Colin. "I got bored, Trint. You was at Eddie's, and there wasn't no one else around, so I come in here."

"What for?" Trinton asked. "What you do all that stuff for?"

"Hey!" Colin protested. "I didn't do none of that. What you think, I'm crazy or something? I just bust in and took a look around, that's all. I never took nothing and I didn't smash up all that stuff. I swear it, Trint, I swear it to God."

"No need, Col," said Trinton. "This ain't your way."

"'Course not," said Colin indignantly. "I do like you do: they go on at me, I make it worse for them. I don't need to smash up desks and things."

"Well, then," said Trinton. "Just tell the man you were out biking, and stuff like that. Grundy ain't going to be able to pin anything on you."

Colin shook his head, and continued to look worried.

"Man, they don't need anything. I got this feeling they going to make things hard for me."

"That's stupid talk, Col," said Trinton. "What reason they got for picking you out? Grundy's interviewing all sorts of kids. I reckon he got a whole list of names, that's all."

At that moment, Ross Marsh strolled into the toilets with his hands in his pockets.

"Hey, Ross," said Trinton. "You been seen by Grundy yet?"

"Yeah," said Ross, "and he sent me to fetch Colin. He's next on the list."

Colin leapt down from the basins and began to crack his knuckles nervously.

"Relax!" Trinton told him. "If he want you so bad, let him come looking for you himself. This is your morning break, Col. You can always tell him you was on the toilet."

"What did you tell Grundy, Ross?" Colin asked.

"Nothing," said Ross, lighting up a cigarette butt. "I wasn't anywhere near here last night. I thought maybe you two did it."

"Get stuffed!" exclaimed Trinton. "Sure, we been in here a few times like you, but we got better things to do than wrecking classrooms. Ain't that right, Col?"

"Yeah," grunted Colin. "Right."

Trinton accepted the lighted cigarette from Ross and took a draw on it.

"Hey," he said to Ross, "didn't Froggy come calling on you last night? He said he was coming for you after we seen him; something about going round to Singh's house."

"Yeah," chuckled Ross. "He got me to go round there with him."

"What happened?" asked Trinton. "Did he see to Singh like he said?"

"You must be joking," said Ross. "He did a lot of talking, the same as always, then some old woman came out and he nearly wet himself. He was off up the road before I could turn round. I tried to get him to go back, but he wouldn't have it."

"What he do then?"

"He went home," said Ross. "That old woman scared him so much he run all the way. You know what he's like: won't ever do nothing on his own."

"Right," said Trinton. "Like the times we been in here at night. Froggy done a lot of talking, but he nearly always had some excuse why he couldn't come with us. And when he did come, he was useless he was shaking so much."

"He was shaking again last night," said Ross. "I reckon Singh would have taken him anyway, even if the old lady hadn't come out. Anyway, I went home and watched telly with my old lady after that: that's what I told Grundy."

Out in the playground, a teacher rang a hand bell to signify the end of the morning break.

"Ain't that just like Froggy?" said Trinton. "He too small even to be called Froggy. Maybe we should call him Tadpole. Or Frogspawn."

Colin was too preoccupied to join in the laughter. His mind was still on his forthcoming interview with Detective Sergeant Grundy. Reluctantly, the boys left the toilets. Mr Jackson met them on the stairs.

"Tremaine," he said, "Detective Sergeant Grundy is expecting you in the medical room – immediately. Adams and Marsh, you go along to your normal lessons. I believe Mr Halligan is awaiting the pleasure of your company in the science room."

"I thought we weren't having normal lessons," said Trinton, "because of the wrecked rooms."

"Some rooms are still out of commission, yes," said Mr Jackson, "but we have enough rooms still in service to provide full lessons for the top two years. Now go where I've told you, all of you."

Not knowing what else to do with them, Colin sat on his hands.

"So," said Detective Sergeant Grundy, "you were on the

street corner with Trinton Adams, helping him sell his papers?"

"Yes," nodded Colin, fixing his eyes on the desk top.

"But you don't know how long for?"

Again Colin nodded.

"Then you cycled home," continued Detective Sergeant Grundy, "but you don't know when? You think you stayed there for about half an hour, but you're not sure? Have I got all that right so far?"

"Yes," said Colin, shifting on his hard seat to relieve the pressure on his hands. It did not escape his notice that the headmaster and Detective Sergeant Grundy had leather-backed chairs with arm rests.

"Right then, Colin Tremaine," said Detective Sergeant Grundy. "What next?"

"Pardon?"

"What next?" the policeman repeated. "You stayed at home for about half an hour, but it could have been more or it could have been less, and then you went out again. Where to?"

Colin thought hard about the question. This was the crunch.

"Come on, sunshine. I'm waiting."

"I'm thinking," Colin explained.

"Thinking?" said Detective Sergeant Grundy sarcastically. "You have to think about where you went? It's last night I'm talking about, son, not last year! Now, where did you go?"

"I went out on my bike," said Colin. "I went looking for Trinton."

"That would be Trinton Adams again, I suppose?"

"Yes. He told me earlier he was going to help his cousin do some electrical work round at somebody's flat. I went out

54

to see if I could find him."

"And did you?"

"Yes," said Colin. "He was round at this person's flat. I found him there and stayed with him; you know, just hung around watching him and his cousin doing this electrical work."

"Whose flat was this, did you say?" the detective asked casually.

"I didn't say," said Colin, looking up at Detective Sergeant Grundy for the first time, "but if you must know, it was a bloke called Eddie."

"Eddie?" asked Detective Sergeant Grundy. "Fast Eddie? Is that what this bloke calls himself?"

Colin nodded and dropped his eyes again.

"Good company these lads keep," said Detective Sergeant Grundy to the headmaster. "He's well known to us is Fast Eddie, very well known indeed."

Trinton winked at Colin as he came back into the science room.

"And what's been keeping you, Tremaine?" asked Mr Halligan. "Found something better to do with your time than attend my science lessons, have you?"

"No, sir," said Colin. "I been in the medical room with the headmaster."

"Ah yes, of course," said Mr Halligan. "Well, you'd better go and sit with your pal, Adams, and copy up the work you've missed. For once, at least, I won't be able to complain when Tremaine and Adams hand in identical work."

For the rest of the lesson, until lunchtime, Trinton and Colin kept their heads down on the back row. When they talked, they did so only in whispers. Mr Halligan could not

remember having such a peaceful lesson for a long time:
perhaps they ought to keep a policeman permanently on
the premises?

At lunchtime a conference took place in the medical room.

"What's your impression so far?" asked Mr Jackson,
eager to discover what developments had taken place during
the morning.

"That's rather hard to say," said Detective Sergeant
Grundy. "Of the lads I've seen, just about any of them had
the opportunity to carry out a break-in like this. Most of
them seem to spend all their waking hours, apart from when
they're in school, out on the streets. I must admit, though, to
being more than a little interested in those two West Indian
lads, Adams and Tremaine."

"I can't say I'm surprised," commented Mr Jackson,
smiling grimly at the headmaster. "I've been convinced for
some time now that those two are riding for a fall."

"It's nothing definite as yet," said Detective Sergeant
Grundy, "just something about their stories. They don't
hang together, you know. For instance, Tremaine says he
spent the evening with Adams, but Adams never mentioned
that when we talked to him."

"I tend to agree with you, Sergeant Grundy," commented
Mr Jackson. "That sounds dodgy to me, too. What do you
intend doing about it?"

"There's not much we can do," said Detective Sergeant
Grundy, "not without some sort of proof that they were
involved; or a confession. Mind you, Adams is a very cool
customer. I don't think we'll get any change out of him. And
this Eddie, whose flat they say they were at, he'd swear they
were there all night if they asked him to. He's as bent as a

nine bob note. So you see the problem. I'll have another go at both of them this afternoon, I think. You never know, one of them may let something slip, but I don't hold out much hope."

"I'd stake a month's salary that it's those two," said Mr Jackson.

"Well," mused the headmaster, tugging at his ear lobe, "I can only hope you're both wrong. I hate to think that any pupils from my school could behave in such a mindlessly destructive fashion."

After school, Nirmal was surprised to find that he was allowed to walk out of the gate without any challenge at all. There was no teasing, no name calling, and no one wanting to fight. Perhaps they had all heard how he had stood up to Froggy James the night before? It was more likely, though, he realized, that they had their minds on the break-in. That was what Trinton Adams and Colin Tremaine seemed to be talking about when he passed them on the bench just outside the side gate. They ignored him completely as he walked past.

"There's nothing for him to see us about now, Col," Trinton was saying. "He's seen us twice and we both told him the same thing. It's obvious they ain't got nothing on us. All we got to do is see Johnny and get him to square it with Eddie. No trouble there: everyone know how Eddie feel about police."

"Thanks, Trint, anyway," Colin said gratefully.

"It's nothing, man," said Trinton. "You didn't do none of this wrecking business, so we didn't do nothing wrong. Like you say, it just makes it easier for you."

"Hope so," grunted Colin. "Anyway, I been thinking,

57

Trint, maybe we should keep out of trouble at school for a bit – just until this thing die down."

"If you say so," grinned Trinton, "but I don't know if I can change my nature quite that easy. It's going to be real difficult."

Froggy James chose that moment to come racing out of the side gates, shouldering some younger children out of the way. His sudden appearance jogged Trinton's memory.

"Hey, Frog," he shouted. "You still taking on all the big men?"

Froggy slowed to a halt.

"They get in my way," he explained, "all these little kids."

"Listen to him," Trinton said to Colin. "He ain't no bigger than a can of beans himself and he calls these kids little. Froggy, we been waiting all day for you to tell us about Singh."

"Singh?" said Froggy. "He won't give me no more trouble. I made sure of that."

"Yeah?" said Trinton. "So how come he just walk past here, same like every day? I don't reckon you did nothing to him, Frog."

"I would've mashed him," said Froggy, "but he got his neighbours on to me. You should have seen him, Trinton, he was scared stiff."

"Funny thing," said Trinton, addressing Colin, "it seems to me Ross told it different."

"Ross?" said Froggy. "He didn't have nothing to do with it. It was me and Singh, that's all, and he won't try anything with me any more. I saw to that."

"There you are," said Trinton, still directly addressing Colin. "I thought Ross must have got it all wrong. You don't see someone as big as Froggy wetting himself just because some old lady come out of her house."

"Yeah," Colin agreed. "Froggy's too hard for that. He's hard, man, hard like . . . hard like . . ."

"Frogspawn!"

Froggy turned bright red, but did not dare say anything in retaliation. No one would take on Trinton and Colin together – not even Ross.

"Hey, hard man," continued Trinton, "you been seen by the police yet?"

"No," said Froggy, "they didn't send for me."

"Funny," said Trinton, "big man like you should be first on the list for any jobs done round here."

"Yeah," said Colin, "why aren't there no posters up for you, you know, public enemy number one."

Froggy had had enough.

"You can laugh!" he shouted as he ran away.

Colin and Trinton did. They both laughed out loud, and rose from the bench, ready to begin another stint on the paper stand.

Mr Jackson watched them go from the window of the staff room. He turned to address the staff who had been called together for an informal briefing on the day's events.

"Those two," he said, jerking his thumb backwards at the departing figures of Trinton and Colin, "I want them. I want them nabbed."

At the street corner, Colin suddenly shivered. Trinton, laying out his papers on the stand, looked concerned.

"What's up, Col?" he asked.

"Don't know," said Colin very quietly. "It just feel like everything going to come down on me all of a sudden."

59

6

The scorebook told the whole story. Lawton Road Middle
School – 56 runs for 3 wickets (innings closed after 20 overs):
Jubilee Street Middle School – 13 all out.

Even taking into account that this was the team's first
fixture, there could be little comfort in it for the players.

Back at school, Mr Bunting gathered the whole team
together in the changing room for an immediate post mortem
on their disastrous debut match.

"I hope that shows you," he said sternly, "just how far
you've got to go before you can call yourself a cricket team.
Our fielding was a disgrace. I lost count of the number of
runs we gave away by sloppy fielding, let alone the chances

we gave their batsmen by dropping catches . . ."

"Yeah," said Ross Marsh, who played in the team as wicket-keeper, "I could have caught them blindfold."

"Quiet!" snapped Mr Bunting. "You were all to blame; it was a shabby, sloppy team display. You didn't look like a cricket team, and you most certainly didn't play like one. Our bowling, after the practice we've put in here in the yard, was very disappointing. You forgot everything I said about line and length and sprayed it down all over the place."

"Singh was rubbish," said one boy. "He was bowling too slow."

"That's just where you're wrong," interrupted Mr Bunting. "I was about to say that Nirmal Singh was the only bowler who tried to carry out my instructions properly. We know they scored some runs off his overs, but at least he stuck at it and bowled accurately. With better fielding, he might even have got some wickets."

Not for the first time, Mr Bunting realized that Nirmal was sitting apart from the rest of the team. He quickly changed the subject to turn everyone's attention away from Nirmal.

"Now . . . our batting. What can I say? You tell me: what was wrong with our batting today?"

It was a short while before the boys understood that Mr Bunting was expecting an answer.

"Come on," he said. "Why was our batting so appalling? Thirteen runs between eleven of you, and five of those from byes!"

"We did have one of our best bats stolen in the break-in," Ross said.

"Do you seriously think that can account for it? Are you actually trying to imply that the theft of one bat so demoralized you all that you couldn't muster more than thirteen runs between you?"

"Well, it didn't help us, did it," Ross persisted. "It was one of our new bats."

"Remember the old saying," continued Mr Bunting: "a bad workman blames his tools. Our equipment was perfectly adequate. The people using it were not. Now perhaps you can see the difference between wild slogging and proper batting technique. At least half of you were out swinging wildly at straight balls. If you had played straight down the line like I taught you, you would have made a match of it instead of enduring this humiliating defeat. Now, do you think you've learnt any lessons today?"

For a while, no one spoke.

"Anyway," he said in a softer voice, "if we can get down to some serious practice and learn from this defeat, I'm sure we'll do better in our future matches. Off you go now, and I'll see you for practice as usual next week."

As they began to leave, Ross turned round.

"Sir," he said, "we'd be a much better team if we had Colin and Trinton. I bet Colin would have got some runs today."

"Yeah," said another boy, "and those Lawton Road kids wouldn't have got so many runs against Trinton's bowling."

Secretly, Mr Bunting could not help but agree with these comments, but he knew it was his duty to comply with Mr Jackson's decision.

"Two players don't make a team, boys," he said, "but if you're so keen to have those two in the team, you'd better get the message home to them that they've got to improve their work and behaviour in school before they can be considered for the school cricket team."

He ushered the last of the boys out of the changing room and locked up.

Every lesson was the same now, thought Colin moodily. As soon as he walked through the door, the teacher, whoever it was, would catch hold of him and sit him in one of the front seats. Even before he had a chance to say a word, they were down on him. And if he did anything to show his anger, like talking to himself or putting on a bad face, the teacher would send him straight out to Mr Jackson. He was the worst of the lot. Ever since that last break-in and Grundy's visit to the school, Mr Jackson seemed to have a smile fixed on his face every time Colin saw him.

"What do you expect?" he would say if Colin complained about the treatment he was getting. "Of course your teachers are picking on you, and they will continue to do so until you accept the standards of behaviour we set for all the pupils in this school. If you feel hard done by, you've only got yourself to blame. Perhaps now you'll realize how it felt for everyone else when you did things that upset the whole school?"

"I didn't do nothing to upset the school," Colin protested.

"Didn't you?" smiled Mr Jackson. "Are you sure about that?"

That smile! All the time, that same damn smile!

Colin spent his time in lessons, when teachers weren't nagging him to work, making up dirty names for Mr Jackson. There was nothing else he could do. It was no use complaining to his parents. His dad always expected teachers to be hard on him; he often told Colin about his own school days in Jamaica, and how the teachers there beat the boys regularly. He used to say: you step out of line, you got to learn to take your punishment!

Nor did he have Trinton to turn to during lessons. Mr Jackson had persuaded the headmaster that Trinton was a nuisance in 4C because the work was too easy for him; he would not have so much opportunity for mischief if he was following a tougher course of studies in one of the higher classes. Consequently, Trinton had been moved to another class away from Colin, which had fixed the smile even more firmly on Mr Jackson's face, or so Colin thought.

At breaks, though, and at lunchtimes, the boys remained inseparable. Trinton was much more cheerful than Colin.

"They'll get fed up with it soon, Col," he said. "It's like a game at the moment, but if you show them they ain't getting on top of you, they soon give it up. All this hard work they supposed to be giving me, it's nothing. We did just as hard in 4C."

"It's Jackson riling me, Trint," said Colin. "That stupid smile, man. It's just like he knows I bust into school, all the time just like he knows."

"You got to take it easy, Col," advised Trinton. "That's how he wants you to be. Listen, he smile at you, you smile back at him. What he going to do then? You tell me, what he going to do?"

Meanwhile, Mr Bunting's cricket practices continued regularly once a week. The headmaster told him that the missing equipment would not be replaced until the insurance claim had gone through, and that was unlikely to be before the end of term. They would have to make do, said the headmaster, with what they had, but he wanted Mr Bunting to know how much he appreciated the time he was spending on the venture.

"Not that I've ever been much of a sportsman myself," he continued, "but I do see the value of teaching children to play the game properly. In a sense, learning to lose with dignity and good grace is the best preparation for life outside school, don't you think?"

Mr Bunting, unable to answer that question, changed the subject.

"Do you think," he asked, "that I might allow Trinton Adams and Colin Tremaine to attend cricket practices again? To the best of my knowledge, they haven't been in trouble for a fortnight, and they might benefit from being shown some sort of trust. It might encourage them to better things."

The headmaster, though, was reluctant to make a decision.

"You'd better see Mr Jackson on that one," he said. "He has rather more day-to-day contact with those two than I have. Put it to him, if you like, and see what he suggests."

Mr Bunting had the feeling that he knew what the deputy head would say, but he put his request to him nevertheless. Mr Jackson smiled and shook his head.

"They are still being sent to me far too frequently," he said. "I know their offences tend to be far more trivial now, but we've still got a long way to go with those two. They're beginning to feel very uncomfortable, you know, especially Tremaine, and that's the way I like it. When they're in that state, you never know when they might let something slip."

"About the break-in, you mean?" Mr Bunting asked.

Mr Jackson, though, said nothing: instead he tapped the side of his nose with his forefinger and smiled.

So practices continued without Trinton and Colin. Mr Bunting got used to dealing with their enquiries and the enquiries of the rest of the team.

"Ask Mr Jackson," he would say, "and, anyway, what makes you think they're good enough for the team?"

Mr Bunting insisted on spending some of the practice time on fielding and bowling exercises, but all the boys wanted to do was to go into a game of knockabout cricket. When he had satisfied himself that they had spent enough time on improving fielding or bowling, he would agree to their requests for a game, but he always set his own special rules for yard cricket: the batsman was out if he hit the ball out of the yard or over any of the buildings.

"Six and out, you mean?" the boys always asked.

"No," Mr Bunting insisted. "I don't want you hitting the ball in the air at all. You must learn to play the ball safely along the ground." It did not seem to make much difference, though. As soon as they had divided into two sides and runs became important, the batsmen would swing at every ball.

"Play down the line," said Mr Bunting, standing in his usual place as umpire. "Try to push the ball into space and take quick singles."

Occasionally, he would stop the game to correct batsmen's mistakes and demonstrate the right technique, but the boys paid little attention.

"Come on, sir," they would say. "We're in the middle of a game."

"You're here to learn," he would reply, "and don't you forget that. Now pay attention . . ."

The team's second match produced a far closer result: Jubilee Street Middle School – 43 runs for 8 wickets (innings closed after 20 overs): Abbeyfields Middle School – 44 for 5 (16 overs). But Mr Bunting knew that this was only because the opposition were much weaker than in the school's first match.

"We did all right, didn't we," the boys said, as they drove back to Jubilee Street in the school minibus. Mr Bunting did not have the heart to point out that they had lost to a poor team; he would keep his reservations about the match to himself.

"Yes," he said, "it was a much closer match. You made a game of it."

"Singh did good today," said Ross. "Three wickets he got."

"No," said Mr Bunting. "Nirmal took two wickets, I think."

"Two caught and one he stumped," said Ross. "That makes three, don't it?"

"The stumping, as you call it, was actually a run out," explained Mr Bunting, "and that goes down in the score-book as 'run out', not as a wicket to the bowler. Still, it was a smart bit of work: a good example of how we ought to be fielding all the time."

"Yeah, and two wickets isn't bad," insisted Ross, sticking to his original point.

"Indeed not," agreed Mr Bunting. "Two wickets for twenty runs is a very good effort in the circumstances."

"It is too many runs, though," said Nirmal. "I tried to bowl straight all the time like you said, but they still managed to hit the ball."

Mr Bunting nodded. He knew very well what had happened. Nirmal had picked up two wickets simply by bowling straight against batsmen who only knew how to spoon the ball into the air. The only Abbeyfields batsman of any note, though, had come out of his crease to Nirmal's invitingly slow bowling and had driven him for three boundaries in one over. Those twelve runs had put the target of forty-four runs for victory well within reach, and the rest of the match had been a formality. If Nirmal bowled like that against the boys of Priory School, who had been coached by an ex-professional cricketer, they would pass a hundred in twenty overs easily.

"How can I make it more difficult for them?" Nirmal asked.

"Have you tried spinning the ball?" Mr Bunting suggested. "That might help."

The idea had been planted in his mind by the Abbeyfields headmaster, who had come out to watch the second part of the game when his boys were batting. He had stood on the boundary edge, puffing at a large, curly pipe and applauding all the runs scored, even when they came from byes or wides. At the end of the match he had come on to the field to pat heads and shoulders.

"Just the right sort of game, eh?" he said, shaking hands with Mr Bunting. "A close match and played in the right spirit. That's the main thing, isn't it? Yes indeed."

Sending the boys inside to orange juice and biscuits, he led Mr Bunting away for a cup of tea in the Abbeyfields staff room.

"I'll tell you who impressed me particularly," he said. "That little Indian feller, the one with the turban affair on his head. You could tell he was spinning the ball, you know."

This had come as news to Mr Bunting, who had been umpiring at Nirmal's end and had watched every ball go through to the batsman dead slow and dead straight.

"Oh yes," continued the Abbeyfields headmaster. "Crafty spinners these Indians, you know. Look at their Test teams – always have two or three first rate spinners, don't they? Yes

68

indeed. Tell you what," he added, jogging Mr Bunting's elbow, "I'm looking forward to the time when we put out an England team with some brown and black faces in it. That'll be the day, eh? Yes indeed."

Back in the minibus, Nirmal looked puzzled.

"How do you spin the ball?" he asked. "Can you show me?"

"I'll try," smiled Mr Bunting. "Next practice, OK?"

Regardless of the result, Mr Bunting was thankful to get through one match at least without anyone referring to the missing players, Colin and Trinton.

As things turned out, Mr Bunting was unable to give Nirmal any lessons in how to spin the ball at the regular cricket practice. It was impossible with so many boys around to concentrate on one individual. Instead, he asked Nirmal if he could come for a special practice on his own the following night.

"I will have to ask my father first," Nirmal said. "I am not sure which shift he will be working tomorrow."

"All right," said Mr Bunting. "Let me know in the morning and if we can fix it up, we'll have half an hour or so in the yard, trying to get you to spin the ball."

Consequently, as soon as the yard was empty on Wednesday night, Mr Bunting took Nirmal into the yard with a box of tennis balls and a block of chalk. With the chalk he drew a wicket on the wall. In front of the wicket he chalked in a batting crease and in front of that he chalked a big circle, in line with the off stump.

"That's where I want you to pitch the ball," he explained. "If you get it right and manage to spin the ball correctly, you should be able to make the ball turn into the batsman's wicket after it has bounced."

They then spent fifteen minutes practising: Mr Bunting demonstrating, correcting and encouraging while Nirmal tried to get it right. He wrapped his fingers wide round the ball and gave it a little extra twist as it left his hand. As he concentrated on trying to spin the ball, he found that he could not control where it would land. Sometimes it would hit the wall without bouncing. Sometimes it would land nearer his own feet than the chalk circle.

When he finally did get one to land in the circle, turn and hit the wicket, he was surprised to hear not only Mr Bunting's words of encouragement, but also a burst of clapping and whistling from the wire netting fence that surrounded the school yard. He turned to see Colin and Trinton leaning against the fence. He had no idea how long they had been watching.

"Ignore them," Mr Bunting advised him. "Concentrate on making that ball pitch and turn. You're doing well now."

After a little more practice Nirmal found that he could pitch the ball consistently into the circle, and most times the ball would turn in and hit the wicket or pass very close to it.

"That's very good, Nirmal," said Mr Bunting. "I think you've got it."

"All very well," Trinton said to Colin in a deliberately loud voice, "but how good would he look if he had a batsman to bowl at?"

"We'll have to see, won't we," said Mr Bunting, "next time we have a school match."

"He ought to be tested before that," said Trinton. "It might be too late in a proper match. You should let Colin and me have a bat against him."

"You know perfectly well that I can't do that," said Mr

70

Bunting. "Mr Jackson has made the position clear to you: you're not allowed to take part in school team activities."

"Until we've admitted to something we didn't do," interrupted Trinton.

"What?" asked Mr Bunting.

"Nothing," said Trinton, "but it's funny how these special rules for me and Colin only started after that break-in."

"Anyway," said Colin, "I don't see no school team practice. It's just you and Singh playing a bit of cricket together in the yard. What harm's it going to do for me and Trinton to join in?"

While Mr Bunting was considering the request, Nirmal spoke up.

"It would be good practice," he said. "If I can bowl properly against Colin, it should give me confidence. He's a good batsman."

"All right then," said Mr Bunting. "Come on, Colin, you come and take the bat. There's the wicket. See what you can do against our new spin bowler. But," he added, "don't imagine that this means I've given you permission to come to team practices again. That's a decision that will have to be taken by Mr Jackson."

Even before he finished speaking, Colin was down in his unusual batting stance, feet wide apart, bat gripped like a club, half raised into the air.

"Right," called Trinton, taking up a fielding position in front of the wicket, "let's see Singh the wonder bowler."

And for the next twenty minutes, the three boys and one adult enjoyed a battle royal between batsman and bowler. Most of the time, Colin was able to move his feet and get to the pitch of the ball so that the spin did not worry him. But, occasionally, when he did not move quickly enough, or

71

when Nirmal gave the ball a little extra flip so that it bit into the playground gravel and turned more sharply, Colin would find himself backing into his wickets in a desperate attempt to stop the ball hitting them. On those occasions, Trinton, who was happily showing his ability as a fielder, would slap his legs and laugh out loud.

"Shame!" he called to Colin. "This boy got you tying yourself in knots. Shame on you, Colin Tremaine!"

"You come see if you can do any better," said Colin, without real anger. "This is hard bowling, man. He's spinning it."

So Trinton tried his luck, and had even less success than Colin. Time and again he galloped out of his crease only to find that he missed the ball completely. He laughed freely at his own failures. He could afford to when there was no one in the yard to watch him, thought Mr Bunting, but how would he react if he had an audience and his reputation was at stake?

"It look slow, man," said Trinton, "but it's really hard to hit."

"What I tell you?" said Colin. "He's spinning it; ain't you, Singh?"

Nirmal nodded and grinned. He was enjoying this practice. Not least, he was enjoying the way that Trinton and Colin were talking to him without a hint of hate in their voices.

"We got to go now," said Trinton. "Or else I be late for my papers."

"I think it's about time we packed up, anyway," said Mr Bunting. "Nirmal is obviously getting tired and his arm is dropping as a result."

"He bowled well, though," said Colin.

72

The smile on Nirmal's face showed how highly he valued Colin's praise.

"Thank you, all of you," said Mr Bunting as they picked up their belongings and left, "but remember what I said. You'll have to wait until Mr Jackson decides that you can start coming to school practices again. And I think it might be a good idea if we kept tonight's little episode to ourselves. Right?"

The boys agreed. They left the school together and walked along the road between the school yard and the council car park. Suddenly Colin broke the silence.

"Hey, Singh," he said. "Froggy James come round your place the other week, didn't he?"

"Oh yeah," said Trinton. "I forgot about that stuff. I ain't hardly seen Froggy the last couple of weeks. He's been away from school more often than he's been here. What he do, Singh, when he come round?"

"He threw stones at the door," said Nirmal, "but when I went out, he stopped and ran away."

"That's Froggy all right," said Colin. "He's soft, you know, Singh."

"I think so," Nirmal agreed, "but Ross Marsh was with him."

"So what?" said Trinton. "Ross won't touch you. If Froggy tries it on, just stand up to him and see what he does then. You just see."

They came to the corner of Nirmal's road.

"I go this way now," he said.

"See you, Singh," called Trinton, already off and running. "Come on, Col, we'll be late for the papers. Don't want nobody nicking them."

Colin turned towards Nirmal for the last time.

"I'll have to practise batting against them spinners," he

said. "You done them well tonight, Singh."

"Come on, Colin," Trinton called again. "The van's dropping the papers now."

Colin stamped down hard on his bike pedals and accelerated away in pursuit of Trinton. Nirmal was left to go the rest of the way alone.

7

Mr Bunting found the message waiting for him on the secretary's desk when he arrived at school the following morning.

Frank—

Please report to my office before morning school

G. Jackson

(Deputy Headmaster)

What did Jackson want? Mr Bunting wondered as he made his way through the school secretary's office to the deputy head's room; it must be something important for it to merit a formal summons like this.

"Sit down, Frank," said Mr Jackson, attending to some official looking documents on his desk. After a moment or two, he turned to Mr Bunting and removed his glasses.

"I didn't want to discuss this in front of pupils of the school," he began in a quiet voice, "so I decided to leave what I had to say until this morning. However, I do feel that you owe me some explanation regarding what took place in the playground last night."

"Pardon?" said Mr Bunting.

"We both know what I'm referring to," continued Mr Jackson. "Last night, against my explicit instruction, you allowed Tremaine and Adams to remain on the premises long past the end of school. And, what is more, you allowed them to take part in your cricket practice after I had explained yet again, less than a week ago, why I wanted them excluded from such activities. Can you offer any explanation for this . . . this act of disloyalty?"

Mr Bunting had to think fast. Should he try to explain? Or should he simply accept his mistake and hear Jackson out to the bitter end? It was clear that the deputy head would not be sympathetic to his point of view. It would be wiser to sit and let the man have his say. The only problem about that was that it made him feel like a schoolboy again, and that bruised his pride.

"I'm sorry," he began, "but it wasn't a real practice, you know. I had just taken Nirmal Singh out for some individual coaching and then, when no one else was around, Colin and Trinton asked if they could join in and help to give him

76

some practice. They had been watching over the fence, you see, and . . . well . . . it didn't seem as though it would do any harm. I did tell them, by the way," he added as an after-thought, "that I wouldn't let them come to full practices until you agreed."

"That's all very well," said Mr Jackson, using his spectacles to punctuate his words, "but you must see this from our point of view . . ." Mr Bunting pursed his lips and listened. With luck, he would be able to get out when the bell went for the start of morning school.

He did not have to wait that long. After Mr Jackson had spent a few minutes going over the same old ground, there was a knock at the door and the school secretary put her head round the door.

"Excuse me, Mr Jackson," she said, "but Mrs James is here. She says she'd like to see the headmaster, only he's out this morning at a meeting, so she'd like to see you instead."

"Mrs James?" repeated Mr Jackson.

"Yes, you know," whispered the secretary, "Alan James in the fourth year: rather a shabby little boy, never looks properly fed. You know who I mean, don't you, Mr Bunting?"

"Oh yes," said Mr Bunting, welcoming the interruption. "I know Froggy James all right, though I haven't seen him about much lately. He seems to have been away rather a lot."

"Very well," said Mr Jackson. "Send her in. I'll see you later, Frank. We'll continue this conversation at a more convenient time."

Mr Bunting left, passing Mrs James on his way out. It

seemed strange to think of such a well-built woman being the mother of little Froggy James.

Out in the yard the fourth year boys congregated around the side gates. Ross Marsh was the centre of attention this morning, as he found a number of willing buyers for the handful of cigarettes which he had "borrowed" from his mother's packet. It was Colin, who had no interest in cigarettes, who spotted Froggy hanging around outside the main door of the school.

"Froggy's back," he announced to the others.

"Yeah," said Ross, turning his attention away from the cigarette buyers for a moment, "his mum come in with him earlier."

"You reckon he's been skiving?" Colin asked.

"Could be," said Ross. "He walked straight past us and didn't say a word when his mum brought him in."

As morning assembly came to an end with a final prayer, the school secretary caught Mr Bunting's eye and beckoned him out of the hall.

"Mr Jackson's office immediately," she said.

"Again?" said Mr Bunting. "What is it this time?"

In Mr Jackson's office, there was barely enough room for three people. Mrs James and Mr Jackson occupied the two chairs and so Mr Bunting had to stand by the door. After making the necessary introductions, Mr Jackson addressed Mr Bunting.

"I think perhaps you can clear this matter up for us, Mr

Bunting. I'm going to ask you some questions, and I'd like you to think very carefully before you answer them . . ."

Mr Bunting nodded dumbly.

". . . first of all, have you, at any time this term, lent young Alan one of the school's cricket bats for his own use at home?"

"Yes," added Mrs James, "about a fortnight or three weeks ago, Alan says it was."

"It can't have been," said Mr Bunting. "I keep all the bats in school."

"Well, that doesn't surprise me one bit," said Mrs James. "I didn't really think he would be just lent a good bat like that. He has been a bit strange lately, and then when I found out about him staying off school, and now this . . . He must have picked the bat up at school one day, I suppose, Mr Jackson. Just you wait till I see him: I'll give him hell for this."

"One minute, Mrs James," said Mr Jackson. "I think there may be more to this than meets the eye. You've brought the bat with you, I believe."

Mrs James produced the bat, wrapped up in an old polythene carrier bag. Mr Jackson unwrapped it and handed it to Mr Bunting.

"Is this a school bat?" he asked.

"Yes," confirmed Mr Bunting. "This is the one that was stolen in that last break-in. Look, it's got the school initials scratched on the back here."

"Break-in?" said Mrs James. "What do you mean, break-in?"

"For the moment, Mrs James, I think it best if we say nothing," said Mr Jackson. "Mr Bunting, I think you should fetch Alan down from his class to my office. No. On second thoughts, I think we'll move to the head's office. And ask the secretary to get Detective Sergeant Grundy on the phone."

"Detective Sergeant who?" exclaimed Mrs James. "What is all this?"

Mr Bunting, though, was already on his way to Froggy's classroom.

They were in the middle of a maths lesson when Mr Bunting came in.

"Hello, sir," someone called out. "What do you want?"

"Be quiet!" their teacher snapped. "You've got work to do. Now get on with it in silence!"

The majority of children in the class took the opportunity for a quick gossip while Mr Bunting explained to the teacher what he wanted. Mr Bunting did steal a glance, though, at Colin Tremaine, sitting by himself at the front of the class. Colin gave him a sheepish grin in return.

"Alan James!" called the teacher. "You're wanted in the headmaster's office immediately."

"Ooh! What you done, Froggy?"

"Been a naughty boy, have you?"

"Yeah. Didn't you see his mam come into school with him this morning?"

"Did she? What's she here for, Froggy?"

Their teacher tried to restore order by threatening to keep the whole class in at morning break, but the flow of comments continued until Mr Bunting led Froggy away to the headmaster's office.

"Hey, Colin," shouted Trinton, as soon as he found Colin in the playground at morning break. "The police are in school again. I saw Grundy coming in about half an hour ago."

"Yeah," said Colin. "I thought they might be. Froggy got called out of class this morning, and he never come back. The way he looked when he went out, you could see he was in big trouble. His eyes were real wide, you know, like he was frightened of what was coming."

"Christ, Col!" Trinton suddenly exclaimed. "Why didn't we think of him before?"

"What you mean, Trint?"

"It's obvious, man, plain as the nose on your face . . ."

Gradually, word spread around the whole playground: Detective Sergeant Grundy was in the headmaster's office interrogating Froggy James. When Mr Bunting came out with the hand bell to signal the end of their break, the whole fourth year was buzzing with rumour and counter-rumour. A group of pupils ran up to Mr Bunting.

"Is it true?" they asked. "Is it true that Froggy's been arrested?"

"Into your classes," was all that Mr Bunting would say.

"Aah, go on, sir, tell us. They say his mam split on him and he's been arrested."

"Into classes," repeated Mr Bunting. "You'll be told all you need to be told when the time comes."

Then, catching sight of Trinton, Mr Bunting called him over.

"Have you seen Nirmal Singh?" he asked.

"Yeah," said Trinton, "I seen him over by the fence earlier."

"Fetch him, please. Tell him to report to me."

"What for?" asked Trinton. "Don't tell me Singh's in trouble? Can't be."

"Less questions and more action, please," said Mr Bunting. "Go and get him."

Trinton swung round and strolled away across the playground. He did not rush around for anyone, not even for Mr Bunting.

Nirmal was flustered and confused. He had never seen the inside of the headmaster's office before, and here he was being brought in to see a policeman. He knew this was a policeman; everybody in the playground was talking about him being in school.

". . . just a few questions, son. OK?"

Nirmal nodded. In his confusion, he had barely heard the man's first words. What was his name? Sergeant Grundy, did he say?

"Now. You remember the night that the school was broken into? About three weeks ago? You remember that particular night?"

"Yes."

"Good," Detective Sergeant Grundy was adopting his gentle voice, the one he usually saved for old ladies whose budgies had disappeared, "now can you remember whether, on that particular night, you saw Alan James after you got home from school?"

"Alan James?"

"You probably know him as Froggy. That's what everyone calls him, isn't it? Did you see Froggy James that night?"

"Yes."

What else could he say? It was the truth. The policeman, though, looked surprised.

"Are you sure?" he asked. "Think hard. Are you sure it was that particular night?"

"Yes, I am sure," said Nirmal. "Froggy came to my house that night."

The policeman and Mr Jackson looked at each other. Then they looked back at Nirmal. Mr Jackson seemed to be about to speak, but the policeman stopped him.

"What did he come to see you for, son? Just a social visit, was it?"

"A social visit?" said Nirmal. "I suppose so. He came to see me about something I had said to him at school. He wanted to fight me, I think."

Detective Sergeant Grundy relaxed, and his expression turned to a broad grin.

"I see," he said. "And did he fight you?"

"No. I went outside to see him and he ran away."

"Why did he do that? If he wanted to fight you, that is?"

"I think it was because the lady next door came out of her house," explained Nirmal, "but I don't think he would have fought me anyway."

"And she saw him, did she?" asked Detective Sergeant Grundy. "The lady next door saw Froggy run away?"

"Yes," said Nirmal. "He went away while she was still there."

"Er . . . is she, you know, is she an Indian lady, your next door neighbour?"

"No. She is white. Her name is Mrs Harris."

"So Froggy came to your house, but he ran away when this lady appeared, and she saw him go? Is that it?"

"Yes. He never came back either, after he ran away."

"Thank you," said Detective Sergeant Grundy. "You've been a great help to us. Can I ask you to help us a little more by not telling your friends about these questions we've been asking you? Keep it to yourself for now, eh? We may want to ask you to put all this down on paper later, but somehow

I doubt whether it'll be needed now."

At lunchtime, Colin and Trinton met Nirmal as he came out of the school canteen. They took an arm apiece, and led him to the quietest part of the playground, out of sight behind the boiler house.

"Now then, Singh," said Trinton. "You tell us what Grundy wanted."

"You mean the policeman?"

"Yeah, he had you in this morning, didn't he? So what did he want?"

"He said I should say nothing about it," Nirmal told them.

"They all say that. It don't mean nothing."

Although Colin and Trinton had let go of his arms, they obviously did not mean to let him go until he told them what they wanted to hear.

"You can tell us," said Colin. "We won't split or nothing like that. We just want to know what's going on."

"He . . . the policeman asked me some questions," said Nirmal. "That's all."

"About what?" asked Trinton. "The break-in?"

"No," said Nirmal. "Not about the break-in, but he asked about some things that happened on that night."

"Such as?" said Colin.

He and Trinton both moved in closer, so that Nirmal found himself backing up against the wall of the boiler house.

"We aren't threatening you," said Colin.

"'Course not," agreed Trinton. "We just like to know what's going on, especially when it involves the police."

They waited. Nirmal looked from one face to the other;

they looked somehow different from the way they had appeared in the playground the previous night.

"He asked about Froggy James," said Nirmal, "about whether he had come to my house that night."

"What you tell him?"

"I told him what happened, that's all," said Nirmal.

"That all he wanted to know?"

"Yes."

Colin and Trinton looked at one another. They seemed puzzled.

"How did Grundy know Froggy went to Singh's house?" Colin asked Trinton.

"Don't ask me," said Trinton. Then, turning to Nirmal, he asked, "Did you tell him?"

"No. He already knew. I just answered his questions."

Colin and Trinton suddenly laughed out loud, and ran away back to the main playground, leaving Nirmal leaning against the boiler house wall.

"There's only one possible explanation," said Trinton. "Grundy's got Froggy for the break-in somehow, and Froggy must have told him he was at Singh's house that night."

"Yeah," Colin agreed. "He must have tried it on as an alibi. How stupid can he get, using Singh like that. He should have known Singh would tell the truth."

"Who cares?" said Trinton. "Main thing is you're in the clear now. If they got Froggy, you can forget all about busting in. Won't be no pressure on you now, Col."

"Right," laughed Colin. "Won't be no one looking for me."

Yet another informal staff meeting was held that same afternoon at the end of school. The headmaster, who had returned from his meeting in the afternoon, gave a brief explanation of the outcome of the day's events. Alan James, having first denied everything, had finally admitted to the break-in. He had acted alone, and had carried out all the acts of vandalism alone. Mrs James had now agreed that her son be withdrawn from the school pending his appearance before the juvenile court; he was, anyway, due to transfer to Upper School at the end of term. Mr Jackson filled in some details: the boy had claimed to have spent the evening at Nirmal Singh's house, but it transpired that he had visited there only briefly and that, later, he had gone to the school to carry out the break-in. This had been verified by Nirmal Singh when he had been questioned by Detective Sergeant Grundy.

"I suppose," Mr Jackson concluded, "that we owe an apology to certain members of the black community. This time, at least, our suspicions have proved groundless. But," he added, "I, for one, have no intention of making any such apologies!"

The children were given no explanation for Froggy's disappearance, apart from being told that he had been transferred from Jubilee Street School. They all guessed, though, the reason for his disappearance. Colin and Trinton became the main ones to benefit from Froggy's confession of guilt. Once the general air of suspicion had been lifted, so was much of the pressure from their teachers.

"You think they might put us back in the same class?" asked Colin, who was finding work much harder without Trinton's help.

"No," said Trinton. "No reason why they should go back on that. I can do the work in my class no trouble at all. It's just the same as you do, really, only the teachers take it serious and give us homework."

"What about cricket, then?" continued Colin. "Will Bunting let us join in that again?"

"Not up to him, is it," answered Trinton. "He said so himself. That all depends on Jackson, and he ain't said nothing to us about it yet."

As things turned out, Mr Jackson did not make the decision. Mr Bunting appealed directly to the headmaster to be allowed to take the two boys back into his cricket squad. The headmaster agreed even before he had heard Mr Bunting's carefully prepared arguments in support of his plea.

"Yes," he said, "I'm sure that it will do them no harm to be given some encouragement after this whole unfortunate business."

And that was that.

Later, when Mr Jackson saw the two boys amongst all the others at practice in the yard, he emerged from the staff room to have words with Mr Bunting. This time, though, Mr Bunting was ready for him.

"See the headmaster," he said before the other could speak. "Trinton Adams and Colin Tremaine have his permission to take part in all my cricket practices and matches from now on."

8

The night before the cricket team's third fixture, against Grove Lane School, Mr Bunting called a special practice. He was pleased to see everyone waiting outside the door when he went out to the changing room after school. He was even more pleased to see that the boys were beginning to acquire the proper kit for cricket. Most of the boys had white plimsolls or training shoes; their shirts, too, were white, or as close to that colour as they could manage. Colin Tremaine even had white cricket trousers. He shrugged off all enquiries about them with the words:

"They were my dad's. My mother's been altering them so they fit me right."

"Doesn't your dad need them any more?" Mr Bunting asked him.

"Nah, he says he don't have time for cricket these days," Colin told him. "He's always too busy working on the house and things."

"Who did he play for when he played?" asked Mr Bunting. "A local team?"

"Yeah, the Casuals, man."

"The Casuals?" said Mr Bunting. "I don't think I've come across that team in local cricket."

"They didn't play a lot of teams from round here," Colin explained. "They all West Indians, see, and they go to play West Indian teams in other towns. I used to go with him sometimes and we stay a whole weekend . . ."

Colin smiled at the memory of it.

". . . beer and rum, you know. All that sort of thing."

Once everyone was out in the yard and ready to start, Mr Bunting gathered them together for a talk.

"Now then," he began, "I want to concentrate on some very basic aspects of cricket tonight."

"You mean like hitting the ball?" asked Trinton, straight faced.

"No," replied Mr Bunting. "I mean what you do after you've hit it."

"That's easy," said Trinton. "Put your head down and run."

And he demonstrated, running on the spot like a character in a cartoon film.

"Precisely," said Mr Bunting, "but there's a lot more to it than that. You aren't going to get far against a good fielding side . . ."

". . . like Priory School, you mean?" someone interrupted.

All the boys had become used to Mr Bunting's regular references to the well-drilled, professionally-coached cricket side put out by the Priory School. Mr Bunting did his best to ignore the interruption.

". . . you won't get far against a good fielding side by simply 'putting your head down and running'. You must learn how to be ready to run, and the correct way to call to your partner. Now, tomorrow's match will give us a good opportunity to polish up this part of our game, so let's make a start now and see what we can do to improve our running between the wickets."

The extra practice, though, was all in vain. Next morning, when Nirmal woke up and pulled back his bedroom curtains, he saw the rain falling. And, in spite of his prayers and those of the rest of the cricket team, it continued to fall all through the morning.

Mr Bunting called the team together at lunchtime to break the news that they were all expecting, but hoping not to hear.

"The match is off, I'm afraid," he told them. "The cricket master from Grove Lane has just been on the phone to me, and he says that, even if it stopped raining immediately, their ground wouldn't be playable this afternoon. Sorry, boys, but this is one game we'll have to miss."

"Are you going to fix it up for another day?" asked Colin, who felt the disappointment even more keenly than most.

"I tried," said Mr Bunting, "but I'm afraid we couldn't arrive at a suitable date. It seems that Grove Lane are booked up with fixtures in the schools' cricket league."

"Cricket league? Why aren't we in that?"

"I didn't know at the start of term," explained Mr Bunting, "that you would be so enthusiastic about playing cricket. I couldn't risk entering a team in the league before I even knew whether we could raise a team."

"Huh! We should have been in it. You never know, we might have won a cup or medals or something."

"Yeah! That would have been smart."

"I beg to differ," said Mr Bunting. "On our form in the last two fixtures, we'd be hard pushed to win an egg cup, let alone the Schools' League Trophy."

"Ah, but it would have been different if it had been in a league. We'd have done better in that."

"Yeah, and if me and Colin had been playing," said Trinton, raising old grudges.

"Let's not go into that again," said Mr Bunting. "It's all finished with now – at least as far as I'm concerned. And regarding your abilities on the cricket field, we still have one last fixture to consider. If you want to prove how good you are, then Priory School are the team to test yourselves against. This is the match that will show you just what there is to cricket. They're not like your Lawton Roads and Grove Lanes, you know. Priory School will be . . ."

"We know, we know," the boys interrupted, "properly dressed, properly behaved and properly coached."

"Which is what cricket is all about," said Mr Bunting.

"That's a matter of opinion," muttered Trinton under his breath.

"I mean," continued Mr Bunting, "that if it's played in the right spirit, with everyone sticking to the accepted rules, then it can be a marvellous occasion to be involved in. You ask your father, Colin. I'm sure he would tell you the same."

Colin, who had occasionally overheard his father talking about such matters, and not in the way that Mr Bunting described, kept quiet.

"Anyway, boys," Mr Bunting concluded. "Today's game may be cancelled, but we'll keep our regular practices going so that we'll be ready for the Priory School fixture. That's the match that matters for us now."

That night Colin and Trinton lugged their bags of kit home after school. The rain had turned into a persistent drizzle that drifted into their faces and made them hunch their jackets round their shoulders to keep dry.

"Great cricket season, this is," said Trinton. "I don't know why we bothered, Col. Honest I don't."

Colin said nothing. He was too busy turning his face away from the wind and rain.

"No rain in Jamaica," Trinton continued, "at least not when they play cricket. I bet they got real good weather there in the cricket season, hey, Colin?"

Still Colin said nothing.

At home Nirmal read an airmail letter from his mother and sisters. He had read it three times already since getting home from school, but now he read it again while his father prepared food for them both. Occasionally his father asked him to read aloud extracts from the letter. Nirmal did as he was asked, reading about villages and people that he had never seen.

As the day of the Priory School match drew nearer, Mr Bunting became more and more concerned that Jubilee Street should put up a good showing in the game. In fact, his main worry was that his school team would perform as disastrously in this match as they had done in their firs fixture against Lawton Road School. He called extra prac tices after school and lunchtime meetings where he explained the laws of the game.

"What have we got to come and listen to all this stuff for?" Trinton asked at one such meeting. "It don't make us play any better, hearing all this about leg before wicket and things."

Mr Bunting, who had just spent fifteen minutes chalking diagrams on a blackboard to explain the operation of the LBW law, tried to answer Trinton's argument. He knew that if it went unanswered, then it would soon be taken up by the rest of the team.

"The main thing," he said, "that I'm trying to do is to make it clear to you when you should appeal for LBW. It would be a little embarrassing when we're playing at Priory School if we were to have all our players shouting for LBW every time the ball hits the pads. As I've tried to make clear to you, there are only two players on the field who should appeal for LBW."

"That's me, isn't it?" asked Ross Marsh.

"Yes," said Mr Bunting, "you, as wicket-keeper, and the bowler, but no one else. Is that understood? When we play at the Priory School, that is how it's going to be. Whatever the result, we're going to look and act like a cricket team."

In the after-school practices, Mr Bunting concentrated on the bowling of Nirmal Singh and Trinton Adams. He chalked a circle in front of the wicket for them and made them bowl ball after ball into the circle. They took it in turns. Nirmal trotted two or three steady paces up to the wicket and lobbed his slow, accurate spinners into the circle. Trinton, on the other hand, ran a full dozen strides before hurtling the ball towards the wicket. He was much less reliable than Nirmal and many of his balls fell short of the circle, rearing up high above the wicket.

"What sort of ball is that supposed to be?" asked Mr Bunting. "I told you to pitch it up close to the wicket."

"They bouncers, man," grinned Trinton. "I bowl them like that to scare the batsmen. It make them nervous when I bounce it up round their ears. I seen Test bowlers doing it – all fast bowlers do it like that sometimes."

"Not when they're playing for my team, they don't," said Mr Bunting. "It's dangerous and unsporting. If you want to get a batsman out, you'll have to do it fair and square while you're playing for Jubilee Street. Now pitch the ball into that circle, well up to the bat. That's how I'll expect you to bowl against the Priory School, so you'd better start getting it right now."

At the start of another practice, Ross Marsh came running out of the changing room to meet Mr Bunting.

"Where's all the kit?" he asked. "I looked in the cupboard just now, and all the pads and bats are missing."

"Don't worry," said Mr Bunting. "I've got them in my car. I'm taking them home tonight to repair them and clean them for the match. They'll be back when we need them, and we can use the old bats for practice in the meantime."

"Funny," said Ross to the rest of the boys, "the kit didn't need cleaning for the other matches. I wonder why it needs doing now?"

"Aah!" said Trinton. "You can't go to Priory School with dirty pads. It's not done, you know."

94

"That's got nothing to do with it," protested Mr Bunting. "The kit needs cleaning regularly. You've got to look after cricket equipment, you know. It's as simple as that."

"So you just happened to choose now to do it?"

"Yes," said Mr Bunting. "It seemed as good a time as any. Now hurry up and get changed. I want you out in the yard for fielding practice in five minutes' time."

"This match better be on tomorrow," said Trinton. "That's all I'm saying. After all the time we spent on these practices, this match better be on."

"Don't worry," said Mr Bunting. "The forecasts are good, and after the way you lot have worked at your cricket over the past few weeks, the sun won't dare not to shine on you tomorrow."

"You wait and see," said Colin. "If it's good weather tomorrow, plenty of sun and that, we'll beat those Priory School kids. I can feel it in my bones."

"Yeah, you see me for speed tomorrow," said Trinton. "I going to knock those wickets down like . . . like a hurricane, man."

"What about Nirmal Singh?" said someone else. "His spinners are really something now. I bet he gets some wickets."

"No chance," said Trinton. "Him won't get a look in. My fast ones going to get them all out."

"Pride comes before the fall, I believe," muttered Mr Bunting.

"What?"

"Nothing," said Mr Bunting. "I was just talking to myself."

"First sign that is: first sign of madness."

"Be that as it may, I would like you to sit down and listen for five minutes," said Mr Bunting. "This is our last meeting before the match and I do have a few instructions to give you. Trinton Adams, that means you as well."

When everyone was sitting down, Mr Bunting took his place at the front of the classroom and began.

"I don't need to tell you how important I think tomorrow's game is: you all know by now how I feel about that. All I want to say now is this – tomorrow, you're not going to the Priory School as eleven individuals. You're not even going simply as a cricket team. Tomorrow you will be Jubilee Street School. You will be representing everyone, all the staff and pupils of this school, and I hope you will remember that."

The members of the team looked down at their feet, or at each other, or into space. They looked anywhere except at Mr Bunting.

"As far as the cricket goes," he continued, "I'm sure that we are as well prepared as we can hope to be. From now on, it's up to you. Just remember this: whatever the result, I expect you to play the game in the right spirit. No nastiness, no intimidation, and, above all, no arguing with the umpires' decisions. Bowlers will pitch the ball well up to the bat, Trinton Adams. Fielders will concentrate throughout the game and will not bicker and shout at each other. Batsmen will curb their natural instincts to knock the cover off the ball and will remember how to call to each other in the correct cricketing fashion.

"Tomorrow," he concluded, "Jubilee Street School will be fielding a cricket team at the Priory School, a cricket team that will understand and follow the finest traditions of the game."

There was no response from the boys. Indeed, some of them looked as though they had not even heard Mr Bunting's words.

"Right," he added, breaking the silence once again. "Does anyone have any questions?"

Trinton looked about him, saw that no one else was going to speak, and slowly raised his hand.

"Good," said Mr Bunting. "What is it, Trinton?"

"Are you going to be keeping us much longer?" he asked. "Only I've got my papers to do tonight."

9

"In!" shouted Mr Bunting, holding open the door of the school minibus. "And be quick about it. We haven't got very long before the match is due to start."

The crush was terrific as the boys clambered over one another to get the best seats in the dilapidated old minibus. Mr Bunting stood back and let the mass of bodies sort itself out. Eventually everyone was seated inside the minibus except Nirmal Singh. He had stepped back from the brawl, and now climbed the step last of all. As he boarded the bus he hesitated and turned to Mr Bunting.

"There is no more room," he said. "All the seats are taken."

"Nonsense," said Mr Bunting. "This is a twelve-seater minibus and there are only twelve of us. There must be room. Now move up and make room for Nirmal."

"I ain't moving for him," said a voice. "Can't you put him up on the roof rack?"

Roars of laughter greeted the remark, and even Nirmal himself smiled.

"Perhaps," said Mr Bunting, when he was able to make himself heard above the noise, "you'd all like to walk to the Priory School? Or, better still, perhaps I should ring them up and say we aren't coming?"

"Get lost! 'Course we're going . . ."

"Then do as I say and make room for Nirmal," snapped Mr Bunting.

Reluctantly the boys shifted up the seat and left a small space by the back door for Nirmal. Mr Bunting closed the door and went round to the driving seat. As he put the key in the ignition switch, he half turned and called over his shoulder.

"One last thing, boys, and this will be the very last: so far today, you've done all I've asked of you. Everyone's got their kit and everyone's smartly dressed. Thank you for that. But remember we're all from the same school, *our* school, so let's forget our differences for once. Please."

With that he switched on the engine and backed the minibus out of the school car park.

"Mr Bunting, I presume?"

As soon as the minibus pulled in through the Priory School gates, the Priory School cricket master came to greet them. He shook hands with Mr Bunting and gestured towards the boys with his free hand.

"This is your eleven, I take it."

"Yes."

"Splendid. Good to see you, boys. Fine weather for cricket, eh?"

He did not even notice that no one answered him.

"Jolly good, jolly good," he continued. "Now then, Jenkins."

A Priory School boy approached from the crowd of onlookers who had gathered to witness the arrival of the Jubilee Street minibus. He was dressed, as were all the Priory School boys, in the uniform of grey blazer and flannels: the blazer decorated with a red badge on the breast pocket.

"Mr Bunting," said the Priory School cricket master, "this is Jenkins, who is skipper of our eleven this year. Jenkins, this is Mr Bunting from . . . er . . . Jubilee Street School."

"How do you do, sir," said the boy, holding out his right hand.

"Very well, thank you," replied Mr Bunting, noticing how quiet his own boys had become in these new surroundings.

The Jubilee Street team had been in high spirits on the journey through town, calling out to passers-by and whistling at girls, but now, on the gravel path outside the main buildings of the Priory School, they stood close together and said nothing. The buildings alone were enough to silence them. The central block, which contained the main class-rooms and offices, had once been someone's ancestral home, and around it were scattered various additional wings, housing science laboratories, art studios, a gymnasium and a swimming bath. But, as well as all this, the team had to put up with ever increasing numbers of grey-blazered Priory School boys turning up on the main drive to stare at them. Trinton Adams found himself clenching and unclenching his fists as he watched the grey blazers laughing and whispering behind their hands.

"Jenkins," said the cricket master, "take our visitors to the pavilion and show them where to get changed. Mr Bunting, you come with me to the staff common room."

He ushered the boys away, and led Mr Bunting in through the big, oak-panelled doors of the main school.

"I'm sure," he said, "you could do with a drop of something before we start this cricket match."

"My God! There's hardly an Englishman amongst them."

The pavilion that Jenkins led the Jubilee Street team to was better than anything they had come across all season, but the dividing walls between the rooms were thin enough for them to be able to hear every word the Priory School players were saying about them.

"We'll probably find that the white ones are Irish or some such thing."

"Jenkins, you never told us we'd be playing the United Nations this season . . ."

In Jubilee Street's changing room, the boys sat on the benches provided, looking at each other and their surroundings: tall lockers to hang their clothes in, wash basins, mirrors on the wall, even soap and clean white towels.

"This is smart," said Colin, slowly nodding his head, "real smart."

Through the wall they heard more laughter and the sound of cricket boots drumming against the floor. Trinton jumped to his feet and began to get changed into his cricket kit.

"I got a feeling," he said, pulling on a white shirt, "that I going to bowl real fast today. Maybe, you know, maybe even one or two bouncers."

"Right!" said Colin, and gradually smiles returned to the faces of all the Jubilee Street players.

"Oh yes, we're very proud of our achievements with these boys," the Priory School cricket master was saying. "Take young Jenkins for instance: a first class boy. He's about to follow his two brothers up to public school, and the eldest boy is going up to Cambridge next term. A quite remarkable family altogether, and all the boys have passed out of the Priory with flying colours."

Mr Bunting nodded or raised an eyebrow when required, and sipped at the glass of sherry that had been pushed into his hand the moment he entered the staff common room.

"Our success rate, you know, is excellent. The head produced some figures the other day on past pupils from the Priory: more than three-quarters of them have gone on to some form of higher education after leaving school. I think that's quite something. Don't you agree?"

"Yes indeed," said Mr Bunting politely.

"Anyway, let's get out to the cricket match, shall we?" continued the Priory School master. "Our boys are rather looking forward to this match. They haven't been beaten by a local school side all season and they're determined to keep their record intact."

As Mr Bunting entered the pavilion to have a last word with the Jubilee Street team, the boys immediately crowded round him.

"They've been saying things," said Ross, acting as spokesman for the others. "We heard them through the walls."

"Who?" asked Mr Bunting. "Who's been saying what?"

"The other team," explained Ross. "When that kid

brought us in here, they were calling out names, you know, nig-nogs and blackies and all that."

"Are you sure?" Mr Bunting asked, but a look round at all the faces in front of him convinced him that Ross was telling the truth.

"Well," he said, "there's nothing we can do about that at the moment. I don't think they'll try anything when their teacher and I are around, so I should try to forget about it if I were you. But if you do want to get your own back, you know how to do it, don't you?"

"Yeah," said Trinton, squaring up and showing his clenched fists.

"No," said Mr Bunting, "that's not the way! You go out there and beat them fair and square on the cricket field. That's the way to put paid to any name calling they may wish to indulge in."

When the Jubilee Street team filed out of the pavilion, they saw the Priory School players limbering up with some fielding practice. Every player in the Priory School team wore white flannels and boots. Most of them had white sweaters, too, decorated with the Priory School colours of grey and red. This was in marked contrast to the plimsolls and training shoes, the trousers and jeans, the buttonless shirts and tee-shirts worn by the Jubilee Street team.

"Never mind," Mr Bunting told them, as he pulled on his white umpire's coat, "you may not look as much like a cricket team as they do, but you can, at least, go out and show them that you know how to play like one. Just try to remember everything I told you in practices."

*

Jenkins, the Priory School captain, won the toss and put Jubilee Street in to bat.

"Lively wicket today," he said, "very green on top. I fancy our chances of getting a few quick wickets here."

Then, turning to the Priory School master, he added:

"We'll open with Gerald from the top end."

Gerald turned out to be a tall, fair-haired boy who opened the bowling off a long, galloping run up. The Jubilee Street opening batsman missed each of the first three balls, and the ball, in turn, missed the wicket by the narrowest of margins. Each time this happened, the Priory School fielders threw up their hands and called:

"Well bowled!"

Gerald, for his part, brushed his fair hair back from his forehead and gave the ball a vigorous rub on his flannels as he marched back to the beginning of his run up.

His fourth ball was a fraction straighter. The Jubilee Street batsman stepped away from the wicket, swung his bat and turned round to see his wickets flattened.

"Oh, well bowled, Gerald!"

The Priory School fielders surrounded their bowler, patting him on the back. He tossed the ball from hand to hand and acknowledged the congratulations.

"If they're all that easy," he smirked, "it'll all be over in no time."

The outgoing Jubilee Street batsman spread gloom and despondency amongst the rest of his team by describing Gerald as the fastest bowler he had ever played against.

"I never saw that one that got me out," he said. "Honest, it's murder batting against him."

During the first few overs, two more Jubilee Street batsmen were bowled out by Gerald. The only runs came from byes and from the bowler at the other end. When the third wicket fell, the scoreboard showed only five runs. While they waited for the next Jubilee Street batsman, the Priory School umpire strolled over to Mr Bunting.

"I'm not really surprised that your chaps are struggling so much," he said. "Most school batsmen have trouble with young Gerald. He's been getting special coaching, you know, at the County ground during his vacations. I'll tell you what, though; if things get too bad, I'll tell Jenkins to take Gerald off and make a game of it."

The next Jubilee Street batsman was Colin Tremaine. He walked to the wicket stiff-legged in pads that were a little too large for him.

"Good God!" exclaimed Gerald loud enough for Colin to hear. "It's another one straight out of the trees."

"Keep your head," whispered Mr Bunting as Colin walked in past him. "Just show them how you can play."

Colin nodded, but said nothing. The look in his eyes, though, was one that Mr Bunting had seen before. It reminded him of the first cricket practice in the Jubilee Street yard.

As Gerald raced in to deliver his first ball to the new batsman, Colin raised his bat to shoulder level. Down came the ball, down came Colin's bat, and back over Gerald's head flew the ball towards the boundary. Colin's feet had barely moved.

Trinton led the applause from the Jubilee Street batsmen who were clustered round the pavilion steps.

"Four runs," he shouted. "Show them power, Col, show them!"

Gerald bowled again. This time Colin gave himself more room by moving out of his wicket. Again the ball flew away to the boundary over the tops of the fielders' heads. The shouts and cheers from the pavilion grew louder. Thirteen runs for three wickets.

Gerald brushed the hair from his forehead. He was not smiling now. Lengthening his run up, he raced in even faster than before. As a result he lost direction and the ball shot down past Colin's legs, beating his bat but beating the wicket-keeper as well. It reached the white sight screen before any fielder could catch it. The Priory School umpire signalled four byes. Seventeen runs for three wickets, and the Priory School fielders fell silent.

And so the game continued. At the other end, two more wickets fell but Colin stood firm. He kept to his favourite stance with legs apart and bat gripped firmly in his strong hands. His biggest hits he saved for Gerald's bowling. Eventually, after hitting a number of boundaries, he ran a quick single and found himself at the bowler's end, right next to Gerald. Colin was overflowing with confidence now, while the sweat stood out on Gerald's pink face.

"You know those trees?" Colin whispered to the bowler. "Those trees you said I come down from? You better watch out, man, because I'm going to hit you back over them next chance I get."

When he got back to the other end, Colin prepared to carry out his threat. He stepped out of his crease and smacked the ball high into the air. It sailed towards the pavilion, and crashed through the branches of a tree next to it.

Trinton snapped his fingers and shouted out loud.

"Six runs, six runs! Show him again, Col."

Forty-three runs for five wickets. The Priory School umpire looked towards the pavilion, and then towards Mr Bunting.

"I say," he said, "d'you think you could ask your boys to control their high spirits? I think the noise may be upsetting the fielders' concentration."

Mr Bunting, though, stood his ground.

"It doesn't seem to be worrying the batsmen," he said, "and that's surely what counts."

At the end of the over Gerald took his sweater and went to field on the boundary. He did not bowl again during the Jubilee Street innings. Gradually Colin ran out of batting partners. Trinton joined him briefly and noisily. Ignoring Mr Bunting's instructions about how to call for runs, Trinton kept up a constant stream of chatter at the wicket.

"Come on, Col," he would shout, "two runs here. Speed, Col, speed!" or: "We'll show them, Col. One more run on the board."

He hit a couple of boundaries himself with lucky swings of the bat before a slow, straight ball rattled into his wicket. He left the crease, grinning, with his bat over his shoulder.

"You got to keep at it, Col," he said. "Show them power!"

Sixty-seven runs for eight wickets. The Priory School umpire sidled up to Mr Bunting again.

"Quite a character, that lad, eh?" he said. "Does he always chatter away like that?"

"Only when he's got something to chat about," said Mr Bunting. "I think he's rather pleased with our performance today."

"Yes," said the Priory School umpire. "Very creditable, very creditable indeed. This other coloured chappie is hitting well. He's certainly got a good eye. Mind you, I can't honestly see him making it as a cricketer: that sort rarely do. His style is really far too crude."

The arrival of another batsman at the crease prevented Mr Bunting from replying, but he remembered with some pleasure the sight of the ball crashing through the branches of the tree by the pavilion.

At seventy-four for nine, Nirmal went out to join Colin at the wicket.

"Oh my goodness me," said one of the fielders, imitating an Indian accent, "what's this one called, Gunga Din?"

"Don't ask me to field too close, Jenkins," said another. "I can't bear the smell of curry."

Nirmal smiled nervously at Mr Bunting as he passed.

"I'm going to try and stay in long enough for Colin to get fifty," he said. "He's got forty-five runs so far."

Nirmal was as good as his word. More by luck than judgement, he kept the ball away from his wicket and out of the fielders' hands. He did not try to score runs for himself, but when he was at the bowler's end he was always alert and ready to run if there was a chance for Colin to add to his score.

Sure enough, when his score had reached forty-nine, Colin found himself facing the bowling.

"One more," Trinton shouted from the boundary. "One more for fifty."

Colin tightened his grip on the bat handle and waited. The ball was a slow one, pitching just in front of his crease. He pushed his foot out alongside the ball and hit it along the ground past the bowler's left hand. A fielder turned to chase, but the ball had reached the boundary before he had gone ten yards. It was as perfect a forward drive as Mr Bunting had seen. All season, in practices, he had tried to teach Colin to play the shot; all season Colin had refused to learn.

As the ball reached the boundary, the Priory School fielders clapped politely. Even their umpire nodded his congratulations at Colin. But away on the pavilion steps,

Trinton led a dance of triumph in celebration of Colin's half century. Nirmal, too, went up the wicket and shook Colin's hand.

In the next over, Nirmal's luck ran out. In trying to keep a fast ball away from his wicket, he pushed it up into the air and a fielder caught it easily. Still, he did not mind: his job had been done. Colin had scored his fifty, and Jubilee Street had reached eighty-two runs all out.

In the pavilion, tables were laid with plates of sandwiches and biscuits and glasses of orange juice, which the teams, keeping to opposite ends of the room, polished off in the fifteen-minute break between innings. Mr Bunting wandered amongst his team, quietening them down and persuading them not to eat too much.

"After all," he said, "you've still got to field. There's a long way to go before you win this match. *If* you win this match, I should say."

"What time is it?" asked Trinton, grabbing another biscuit from the fast disappearing pile.

"Getting on for three-thirty," said Mr Bunting.

"That's fine," said Trinton. "We can get them all out, and I'll still be in time to do my papers."

"Didn't you fix up someone to do it for you?" asked Colin.

"No," said Trinton, "I need the money, man. If I get someone else to do the papers, I got to pay them and I can't afford that."

"That's enough biscuits," said Mr Bunting. "Just take your fair share, boys, and don't be greedy. Remember where you are . . ."

*

As they went out for the start of the Priory School innings, the Priory School umpire told Mr Bunting that there would be more spectators for the second half of the match.

"It's a tradition at the Priory," he said, "that the school is allowed out at three-thirty when our first eleven are playing at home. I think it adds to the atmosphere of the occasion – don't you? – to have some enthusiastic and appreciative spectators on the boundary edge."

As long as they're supporting the right side, thought Mr Bunting, but he made no comment.

The Jubilee Street team came out to field, looking determined and angry. Ross explained why when he walked past Mr Bunting.

"They were at it again," he said, "when you went out of the pavilion. Saying things, making comments loud enough for us to hear."

"What sort of things?"

"The same as before, you know, about the black kids and that. They said something, too, about it looking like a chimpanzees' tea party when we were eating in the pavilion."

"Did any of our boys say anything?" asked Mr Bunting.

"No," said Ross, "but their batters had better watch out when Trinton's bowling. He's ready for them."

Mr Bunting turned to look at Trinton. He was standing, waiting to bowl, and absolutely still. The rest of the Jubilee Street team had already taken up the positions given to them, and Trinton slowly rubbed the ball against the leg of his trousers. His face betrayed no expression, but the stillness of his body communicated his feelings as well as any words. He was ready.

His first ball hit the wicket-keeper's gloves as the batsman's feet were still moving into position to play the ball. His second ball did the same. As he walked back to bowl again, the first Priory School spectators appeared on the boundary. Amongst them were members of staff, wearing long black gowns. They were just in time to see Trinton's first bouncer. He pitched the ball a little shorter, and it reared up past the batsman's chest. Ross, the wicket-keeper, had to jump to stop it from going for byes.

"I say!" muttered the Priory School umpire.

"Well bowled," whispered Mr Bunting to himself.

The last three balls of the over were equally fast. The last one rapped the batsman sharply on his pads.

"HOW'S THAT?" roared the whole Jubilee Street team.

"Not out," said the umpire briskly, "and that is over."

More and more grey blazers appeared on the boundary. The Jubilee Street fielders looked round and listened to the buzz of conversation as they changed positions between overs.

"It makes me nervous," said Nirmal, who was to bowl from the other end. "I'm not used to so many people watching me bowl."

"Don't you worry," said Trinton, who was fielding close to the bowler. "The more the better: there won't be no argument then when we give them a good licking."

Despite these words of encouragement, Nirmal was too nervous to bowl properly in his first over. He could not find his rhythm and the batsmen took full advantage of his inaccuracy. From a variety of scoring strokes they accumulated eight runs. They and their supporters were in much better heart by the end of the over, when Nirmal handed the ball back to Trinton.

"I'm sorry," he said. "Perhaps someone else should bowl?"

"No," said Trinton, "you're the best we got. You'll be all

right when you settle down. You just got to imagine you're back in the yard at Jubilee Street bowling into that circle."

This time Trinton produced a bouncer as his first ball of the over. It reared up to head height and, as the batsman lifted his bat to fend it off, the ball struck his glove and dropped on to his wicket.

"How's that?" shouted Trinton.

"Out," said the umpire, "but it's a somewhat ungentlemanly way of taking a wicket."

Trinton shrugged.

"Just so long as he's out," he said.

The next batsman, by contrast, received a fast full toss that went straight between his bat and pad, and lifted the middle stump clean out of the ground.

"Anything wrong with that ball?" Trinton asked the umpire.

At the end of the over, the scoreboard showed eight for two: seventy-five runs needed for victory.

By following Trinton's advice, Nirmal found that he could control his nervousness. As he ran in to bowl, he imagined the chalk circle in the yard, and it became quite easy to make the ball bounce just in front of the bat where he wanted it to. Runs were not so easy for the batsmen to come by now; they had to concentrate on stopping the ball from spinning into the wicket.

"Good bowling," said Trinton at the end of the over." See what I mean?"

During the next few overs, the batsmen had several lucky escapes. Trinton got the ball past the bat a number of times, but each time the wicket was left intact. Occasionally the ball hit the batsmen on their legs and thighs. Trinton said nothing. Occasionally he bowled too fast for his own wicket-keeper and the resulting byes were added to the Priory score.

Twice, too, the batsmen hit the ball into the air, trying to score runs off Nirmal's spin bowling. Neither time, though, did the ball go close enough to a fielder to be caught. Gradually the score rose and the batsmen's confidence increased. Twenty-three for two, the scoreboard read: sixty runs still needed, and eight wickets to fall.

It was becoming clear that Trinton had put too much into his opening overs. After half a dozen, his bowling slowed down enough for the batsmen to begin attacking him. The Priory School supporters began to sense victory as the score mounted. Forty followed thirty on to the scoreboard and there were still only two wickets down. Another bowler replaced Trinton, but Nirmal continued to bowl tightly from his end. Every ball was dropping on the spot now, and some of them were spinning enough to cause difficulties for the batsmen.

Nirmal, though, was puzzled. He knew he was bowling better now than he had done in any of the school matches or practices to date, and yet he was not getting any wickets. Usually he only had to wait for the batsmen to lose patience, but these batsmen were happy to push the ball back to him and score runs off the bowler at the other end. He would obviously have to do more than bowl into the circle, he decided.

"Right," he said to himself at the start of the next over, "I will have to fool this batsman to get him out."

The first four balls he tossed up even more slowly than usual, right in front of the bat. The batsman pushed them back to him without trying to score. For the fifth ball, though, Nirmal changed his grip on the ball. He ran up to the wicket in exactly the same way as usual, but wheeled his arm over a little more quickly.

The batsman, expecting yet another slow ball, lifted his bat a fraction too late and the ball hit his wicket before he noticed that it was different from the previous four balls of the over. Forty-four for three: thirty-nine runs needed.

"Good stuff!" Trinton said. "You got him easy, Singh. What did you do?"

"Nothing," said Nirmal. "I didn't try to spin it at all that time."

From then on, Nirmal experimented in every over. Sometimes he bowled slower, sometimes quicker. Most of the time he tried to spin the ball as Mr Bunting had taught him, but occasionally he changed his grip on the seam to see what would happen. When things went wrong, the batsmen scored runs, but more often than not he held the upper hand. In rapid succession, he bowled out three more batsmen and two more were caught hitting slower balls into the air: six wickets in all. The scoreboard showed sixty-seven for eight, and the grey blazers fell silent again.

The only batsman to survive Nirmal's onslaught was Jenkins, the Priory School captain. With only sixteen runs to get for victory, it was essential that he should stay at the crease.

Trinton, though, had other ideas.

"I'll bowl again," he said. "I'm ready now. This is the one I want to get out."

There was no arguing with him. The fielders took their positions and Trinton took the ball. For a second or two, everyone on the pitch was perfectly still. Jenkins took his stance. Trinton stood at the end of his run and shone the ball against his trousers. All the fielders waited, hands at the ready. Trinton ran in to bowl.

Another bouncer! Jenkins ducked and the ball flew over his head. The wicket-keeper, too, missed the ball and the batsmen ran two byes before a fielder retrieved the ball. Thirteen runs still needed.

"I hope we're not going to see too much of this," the Priory School umpire said to Mr Bunting.

"Too much of what?" asked Mr Bunting.

"This dangerous bowling," said the Priory School umpire. "It's becoming rather too frequent for my liking."

Mr Bunting folded his arms.

"Shouldn't we get on with the game?" he said.

Trinton bowled again to Jenkins, who pushed the ball for a single. Thirteen to win. With the easier batsman to bowl at, Trinton redoubled his effort. He produced the fastest ball of the afternoon to shatter the batsman's wicket. One of the bails landed far beyond Ross and the slip fielders.

"Out!" shouted Trinton. "Man, you – are – out!"

Trinton and Colin hugged each other as the Priory School umpire rebuilt the wicket. He was distinctly unhappy.

"Victory at all costs," he muttered. "That's not what cricket is about, you know. There's much more to the game than that!"

Thirteen to win or one wicket to fall. Nirmal took the ball. His nervousness returned as suddenly as it had left him. His fingers could barely grip the ball. He tried to concentrate on the chalk circle, but all he could think of was the scoreboard. Seventy runs for nine wickets, it read.

The ball pitched half way down the wicket. Jenkins stepped out and gleefully pulled it to the boundary for four runs. The cheers rose from the grey blazers. Nine runs to win.

Yet again the ball fell short. Yet again Jenkins drove it to the boundary. Five to win. From being the destroyer who had captured six wickets, Nirmal was fast becoming the easy paced bowler who would give away the few runs that Priory School still needed.

Trinton brought him the ball.

"Just put it in the circle, Singh," he said. "Don't try anything new now. I know I can get this last wicket if you just finish this over without giving them any more runs."

Somehow Nirmal managed to pin Jenkins down for the rest of the over. Trinton took the ball and smiled.

"I'll get this bloke now," he said. "You see."

Nirmal went out to his usual fielding position close to the boundary and the grey blazers. Trying to ignore the noise from over his shoulder, he concentrated his attention on Trinton and the number eleven batsman who was facing him. Again it was a very fast ball that just caught the edge of the batsman's bat and ran away past the slips. The batsmen took one run, and Jenkins found himself at the receiving end. Four to win. Trinton ran in to bowl. Jenkins had obviously decided that the time had come to do or die. Even before Trinton bowled he was moving out of his crease. He hit the ball on the rise towards the boundary.

Everyone turned, batsmen and umpires included, to follow the flight of the ball. On the boundary's edge, Nirmal stood still as the ball flew straight towards him. He did not have to move; it would drop straight into his hands. Please, he prayed, please let me hold it . . .

"It's a four!" shouted the grey blazers. "He's dropped it, he's dropped it!"

Indeed he had. If he lived for a century, Nirmal would never understand how it had happened. The ball had dropped straight through his waiting hands and had thumped against his chest. The next thing he saw was the ball trickling across the white line that marked the boundary edge. It was four runs, and the Priory School had won. The grey blazers set up a roar of applause as Jenkins raised his bat high in the air. The Jubilee Street players gathered round Trinton, their faces mirroring their anger and disappointment.

"Go off together," Mr Bunting told them, "and hold your heads up. You've got nothing to be ashamed of."

The Priory School umpire collected the bails and caught up with Mr Bunting. He insisted on shaking hands.

"An excellent finish to the game!" he said. "That was the closest match we've had against any of the local schools. It's a pity, in a way, that either team had to win."

"Yes," said Mr Bunting.

"I'm sorry, by the way, that I had to speak to your fast bowler," the umpire continued, "but I do like to see school-boy cricket played in the proper spirit."

Mr Bunting could no longer contain himself.

"The proper spirit?" he said. "Before you criticize my boys for anything they have done on the field, I suggest you examine your own boys' behaviour, and, in particular, their treatment of their visitors. All I can say is this, if they've been playing in the proper spirit, as you call it, we'll carry on playing it our way, thank you very much!"

Mr Bunting and the Priory School cricket master stood and looked at each other as the spectators on the boundary edge applauded the Jubilee Street team into the pavilion.

Ross threw his wicket-keeping gloves on to the bench.

"Singh!" he shouted. "If you hadn't dropped that catch, we'd have done it. What did you have to drop it for, you stupid . . ."

"Shut it, Ross," said Trinton. "You just shut your

mouth! All right, Singh drop the catch and we lost, but we wouldn't have got nowhere near winning if he hadn't taken all them wickets. So if anyone got anything to say to him, they better say it to me first."

"And me," added Colin, at his friend's shoulder.

After which nobody spoke another word for many minutes.

Gradually, though, the tension disappeared. By the time Mr Bunting appeared in the changing room, the whole team was laughing as Trinton recalled incidents from the game.

". . . man, you see that fast bowler's face when Colin hit the ball into the trees?"

"Yeah," said Colin, enjoying the memory of it. "I told him I was going to do it."

"You what?"

"I told him. 'See those trees?' I said. 'I'm going to hit the ball over them!' "

"You said what?"

The noise of the team's laughter filled the whole pavilion.

10

The minibus left the Priory School without ceremony. Mr Bunting shook hands with the Priory School master, Trinton shook hands with Jenkins. Very little was said.

"Perhaps we'll see you next season?"

"Perhaps."

They struggled back through town, getting caught up in the early evening rush hour. While they edged their way along the High Street, someone from the back of the minibus asked:

"Do you think the school will have a cricket team next year?"

"That all depends on whether anyone comes to the

practices," said Mr Bunting. "If I can get a group of kids as keen as you, we'll have a team all right. And if they play half as well as you did today, they'll be a damned good team, a team to be proud of."

Back at Jubilee Street, Mr Bunting ushered them out of the minibus.

"Home you go," he said. "I'll see you all tomorrow."

When the last boy had left the school yard, he began to hump the cricket kit from the car park to the games cupboard in the changing room. The bag seemed much heavier now, and his arm ached from the strain of carrying it. When he reached the changing room he had to rest on the bench before stacking the kit away in the cupboard.

In the kitchen of his house, Colin unpacked his kit bag. He took out the crumpled flannels and handed them to his mother.

"I will have to soak these, Colin," she said. "How else you expect me to get the grass stains out? Beats me how you get in such a mess just playing a game of cricket."

"Leave the boy be," said his father. "What's a little dirt on his pants compared with fifty runs? Fifty runs, woman! Just think of that . . ."

Nirmal turned his key in the door. Even before he stepped through the doorway he could hear the voices from the back room. His uncles were there with his father. His father beamed as he walked in.

"Why do you look sad?" he asked.

"We lost the cricket match," Nirmal explained. "It was a close game, but we lost."

"Never mind," said his father. "There is an airmail letter on the table. Read that; no doubt it will cheer you up."

Nirmal snatched the letter. He read the first few sentences and broke into a smile.

"My mother," he said, "she is coming home!"

Back in the Jubilee Street car park, Mr Bunting searched his pockets for his car keys. He found them but, just as he was about to unlock the car door, he hesitated. Instead, he put the keys back in his jacket pocket and walked out of the car park.

When he reached the main road, he looked all around until he saw what he was looking for. On the far side of the road, on a street corner between the social security offices and a gents' outfitters, there was a newspaper stand. Behind it, with his pile of evening papers, stood Trinton Adams.

Mr Bunting made his way across the road, dodging the traffic.

"Hello," he said when he reached the newspaper stand.

"Hi," said Trinton. "You want a paper?"

"Oh...yes..." said Mr Bunting, digging into his pockets for loose change. Trinton handed over the paper, but Mr Bunting folded it up and tucked it under his arm without looking at it. There was a brief pause before Mr Bunting spoke again.

"It was a good game today," he said. "We nearly won it. If only Nirmal Singh had taken that catch ..."

Trinton shrugged and shook his head.

"You can't blame him," he said. "That would have been a hard catch for anyone to take, especially with all those Priory School kids out on the boundary. I bet they put Singh off."

"I suppose that's true," Mr Bunting agreed. "I hadn't really thought about that aspect of it, I must admit."

There was another silence. Trinton looked past Mr Bunting and jiggled a handful of coins.

"Well," said Mr Bunting at last. "I suppose I'd better be going. You'll be wanting to get on with selling your papers."

"Yeah. I get a lot of customers about now."

"I suppose you do," nodded Mr Bunting. "Goodbye, then. No doubt I'll be seeing you in school in the morning."

Trinton said nothing. He was busy now counting the loose change in his money tray. Mr Bunting, though, did not go. He still hovered in front of the newspaper stand.

"Trinton," he said, "I know this has been a hard term for you in many ways – well . . . I hope that's all behind us now – but I would like to say, before it's all gone and forgotten, I'd just like to say . . . thank you."

Trinton stopped counting his money. Slowly he looked up at Mr Bunting.

"What for?" he asked.

But Mr Bunting was already turning to cross the road.

"Let's just leave it at that," he said. "Thank you."

And, without another word, he went.

What did the man mean, Trinton thought, what did he mean by saying that? Thank you? Thank you for what? He hadn't done anything for Mr Bunting, so what was there for the man to thank him for?

Anyway, he didn't have time to worry about such stuff. Why should he have to figure out what went on in teachers' minds? After all, there were plenty more important things to think about. For instance, hadn't he just had a message from his cousin Johnny to say that Fast Eddie wanted him to work that night, carrying equipment and fixing up speakers for the sound system? The thought of working for Eddie brought a ready smile to Trinton's face, as he began once again to count the coins in his money tray.